GABRIEL'S BALLOON

GABRIEL'S BALLOON

by

Hope Michelle Ayers

MILL CITY PRESS

Mill City Press, Inc.
2301 Lucien Way #415
Maitland, FL 32751
407.339.4217
www.millcitypress.net

Printed in the United States of America

ISBN-13: 978-1-5456-7885-5
LCCN: 2019915099

DEDICATION

This book is dedicated to Chelsea, my Daughter, my Muse, the one who loved me through the happening and the writing of <u>Gabriel's Balloon</u>. Your heart, my love, is amazing. More than magic, you are my hope and my air, if ever I wish, if ever I breathe.

TABLE OF CONTENTS

PROLOGUE

M ost moments in life are non-descriptive. They pass us by, move into the next one, mostly unnoticed. They simply are the passing of time. Yet, every human being, every life lived, will endure moments that are so poignant, so filled with thought and emotion and action, that they do more than just merely pass time. They become the defining moments in one's life. The happiest, the most successful human beings are the ones who, during the same time span of existence have more defining, more noticeable moments than the other people in their personal lives, than the members of their communities, than their fellow countrymen, than citizens of the remaining world, even. The multitude of their defining moments create extraordinary situations and monumental outcomes, so much so that society elevates them above the common masses and history occurs through their achievements and accomplishments. They are the very special people, those who, for whatever reason, utilize more moments to define their existence rather than to simply just pass time away.

No one knows why they are the chosen ones, the ones destiny, fate,–dare I say–God has determined to bear the torch of existence of mankind, but their presence is undeniable. We know them when we see them. We hear about them. We read about them. We write about them. We talk about them.

Since the day he was born, people talked about Gabriel Loveman. From the start, his uniqueness was apparent. He had come into this world as a second son, a little brother, his mother having endured several miscarriages between the births of her children, horrible abortions that occurred when she was well into her second trimester. Without hint or warning, in her sleep, or sometimes as she labored in the field, Rosalee Loveman would experience one sharp pain and with one slight push or grunt on her part, her fetus would prematurely and fatally expel from her. As a field hand on a cotton plantation the only medical care she received was at the hands of the midwife who, on each occasion, could only shake her head in bewilderment. Although she never shared her fear, the midwife was almost certain the Lovemans were cursed and would never again experience the joy and the miracle of the birth of a healthy child. Even if the midwife had so much as suggested her concern to the Lovemans, her opinion would have fallen on deaf ears. Out of the earnest need to not endure the same magnitude of heartbreak they had suffered the first time she miscarried, John Loveman and his wife, Rosalee, had rationalized that the unexplained losses were not deaths of their unborn children but rather physical components of the spiritual revelation of a precious child yet to come, a child just as special and blessed as their first born, a child so unique that the making of him or her required more than one pregnancy. And so whenever Rosalee miscarried, they did not trouble themselves with sadness or mourning. Instead, they viewed each pregnancy, which oddly enough lasted longer and longer each time, as a preparatory foreshadowing of the one that would bring forth into the world a child so exceptional, upon his arrival, the stress of the physical and emotional strife required to produce him would soon be forgotten.

When Gabriel Loveman was born, John and Rosalee's belief was confirmed and the midwife's fear disproved. From the second he exited his mother's womb, eyes wide open and alive with wonder, the Lovemans considered themselves the recipients of a blessing well worth the anticipation they had endured over the seven years between the birthdays of their sons Benjamin and Gabriel.

As a baby, his cry was deliberate and rendered only when necessary. If he was not hungry, wet or soiled, he remained quiet. His quietness, though, was reassuring, not alarming. From the time he was born, Gabriel remained deep in his own thought and while he did not mind being held and though he enjoyed the thrill of a tickle or the comfort of a sweet caress from his mother, he seemed most at ease when he was on his own. Whether he was lying in his handmade crib, which was actually just an oversized woven basket or on a tattered sackcloth under the big oak tree that served as his babysitter as his folks labored in the field beside it, Gabriel was a content and peaceful baby. His large, engaging eyes held hope and wonder and, on sight, older folks spoke of how amazing it was to see a babe look them in the eye with so much understanding. As a little boy, he quickly mastered the ability to read and from the age of five, Gabriel was able to memorize whatever he observed or heard. He was indeed a wondrous child and quite often the subject of many conversations held by folks who lived on the Peterson Plantation and neighboring farmlands.

He was described early on as a wise, gifted, and an extraordinary child, a child destined to become a great man and everyone who lived alongside him and his family in the area of the plantation referred to as the "Quarters," where all of the field laborers lived, were all fully aware of his extraordinary intellect, his special and unique brilliance. By the time he turned eighteen years old, many of the predictions about him had come to light. He had grown to be a tall man, standing nearly six and a half feet and, though he wasn't thin enough to be described as boney, he was gaunt, to say the least. He was a handsome young man, with his mother's rich caramel brown skin and his father's facial features, huge piercing eyes, a sharp nose and lips that were perfectly full and pouty. Gabriel's aura was a very quiet one and although he never apologized or shied away from his exceptional way of learning and retaining information, his subtle manner was a balancing factor. Rather than being intimidated by him, his friends and neighbors were drawn to him and he was well liked. He wasn't known to show his playful side often, especially in the past few years, but when he did, his smile was infectious and his laugh was hearty. Yet, by the time he was considered a grown man, Gabriel Loveman was as sad as he was brilliant. And with good reason.

Chapter One

HOPE AND HATE

G abriel Loveman was enjoying a leisurely day off, a rare and
much needed break that hardly ever happened for him and
everyone else who labored in the fields of the Peterson Plantation,
when, suddenly, his life changed forever, again.

The knock at the door was so loud that he awoke from his nap
with a start. Given the pleasure of a pastime as precious as an afternoon nap and especially given the sheer relief that particular nap
was providing him, Gabriel was secure in his decision to ignore the
knocking and to maintain the most comfortable position possible on
his makeshift bed when he was disturbed again, this time by rapid
pounding even louder than the knocking before. He jumped to his
feet thinking that if he quickly told whoever it was banging on the
shabby door that whoever he or she wanted to see was not there, perhaps he would be able to restore his nap before he was too awake to
fall back asleep. But as soon as Gabriel saw the somber expression
on his elderly neighbor's face, Gabriel knew his afternoon of rest was
over. He had been sent for by Mr. Robert and Eli, the man charged
with delivering the message, knew that the more time between the
beckoning and Gabriel's arrival, the more likely the both of them
would suffer a harsh redress from the man who controlled the lives

of everyone who lived on the Peterson Plantation. Gabriel's poor neighbor, Eli, had run all the way down the long, winding path from the big yellow mansion on the hill overlooking the fifty acre farm and had knocked as hard as he could, all the while fearful that no one would be home at Loveman cabin. He pounded on the door knowing that most of the laborers had gone off to one of the remote fields for a worship gathering, another rare instance that only occurred when, for whatever miraculous reason, Mr. Robert allowed them to take time off from the fields. By chance, this particular afternoon, Gabriel had decided to remain behind. Pushing the door open, he could not help but notice the look of relief on his neighbor's face and as the older man stepped into the front room of the tiny cabin, Gabriel paid close attention as Eli drew a deep breath and relayed the demand.

"Gabriel, you gotta get up to Mr. Robert's right away now. He say for you to come right directly. Don't waste no time. He say he got something for you. And you know what it is."

Out of breath from running so fast, he paused a quick bit before continuing. "Get up there right now Gabriel, fast as you can! I don't want no trouble out of that wicked rascal. Not for you and certainly not for me!"

Before he responded, Gabriel cleared the sleep from his throat. Gabriel Loveman always spoke clearly. Any word spoken by him was accompanied, always, with deliberation and precise diction. He looked his neighbor straight in the eye, to show his respect and appreciation of the man's plight.

" I don't want any trouble either Mr. Eli. Thank you for telling me and don't worry. I won't waste any time."

Gabriel's neighbor obviously had more than exerted himself in order to get the message to him as quickly as possible and so, despite the urgency of the matter before them, he was still mindful to remember his manners.

"Can I get you a drink of water? Do you need anything before I go, Sir?"

As he caught his breath, collected himself and shook his head, Eli suddenly considered just exactly who he was delivering the message to and right away, his heart was overcome with fear and worry.

"You gone be alright Gabriel? You want me to go with you, son?"

"No sir. But I most certainly would appreciate it if you would watch out for my folks. If I'm not back when they return from worship, let them know where I'm off to. And please sir, make sure they don't worry. Let them know that I am just off to handle an errand for Mr. Robert and I will be home before sundown."

"I'll make sure they don't worry theyselves, son. Your poor Ma and Pa done worried theyselves long enough now. Yes sir, they done put in my time and plenty other people's time with they worrying. I'll let them know where you be without getting them all stirred up."

With that, Gabriel reached for his field hat and brushed past his neighbor. One quick hop off of the makeshift porch to the cabin and he was headed up the pathway to the antebellum mansion that housed the Peterson family.

The ten minute uphill walk to Mr. Robert's house was reduced to three because Gabriel could not help but run as fast as he could all of the way. Still, he didn't want to look like some breathless, overly anxious fool when he arrived at the Peterson's front door, so he slowed down and walked the long driveway, regaining his composure by the time he stepped up to the front door. As he waited to receive the customary nod from the butler, the nod that sent him around to the servants' entrance of the first level of the three story manor, Gabriel reminded himself to remain calm and to keep his composure. He had to control his emotions, no matter what happened once he was inside the house he had hardly ever seen up close but spent most days of his life working to support and maintain.

The door to the servants' entrance was already being held open for him. He had been sent for and was expected, so there was no need for any announcement or exchange of words. As he made his way down the long hallway that led to the great room of the antiquated home that had housed the Peterson Family for the last one hundred years (although it had been rebuilt after it was partly destroyed during a fire in the midst of the Civil War), his heart beat so hard, so rapidly, Gabriel thought it would jump right out of his chest. He couldn't think straight, let alone him prepare himself for a conversation with Robert Peterson.

Whether in the form of a message, an instruction, a commentary or a declaration, whenever Robert Peterson spoke, his words usually led to another human being's injury. At best, one could only hope and pray that the injury would only be an emotional one and that no tangible, physical harm would result from Robert Peterson opening his thin-lipped mouth and speaking the evil lurking in his twisted, demented mind. Arriving in the parlor, with his composure barely in tact, Gabriel found himself facing the man who had demanded his attendance, a man who exerted authority over every single person who lived on the Peterson Plantation, a man whose words and acts controlled every component of the lives of those burdened with the misfortune of living and working on his property.

Robert Peterson could easily be characterized as the one of the most evil white men the whole South over. He seemed to live life as if he had been assigned by the devil himself to spend all his days demonstrating to the rest of the world exactly how, when and why to be cruel. Simply put, he was mean, mean to his wife, mean to his friends, mean to his fellow church members, even mean to his minister. Most of all, he was exceptionally mean to the people of color, the descendants of slaves who served as his entire workforce, save the very few poor white men he used as field managers. His disdain for the people who lived on and worked the fields of the vast farmland known near and far as the Peterson Plantation was clear from the way he refused to pay them for their labor, though slavery had been abolished for decades, clear from the way he often ordered savage beatings of the women, usually in the presence of their husbands and children and even more clear from the way he sometimes commanded the killing of the men, often while their families and neighbors were watching. Robert Peterson was a monster in the flesh and the day he called Gabriel to his house his demeanor was the same as always, bitter, mean and dark.

As Gabriel stood waiting for Robert Peterson to speak, he knew the words he would next hear would indeed cause him harm. The extent of that harm depended on the contents of the item that now existed between them, the letter that Robert Peterson was tactfully tapping on the palm of his hand, his large reddened hand, which was slightly extended toward Gabriel's face. The envelope had already been opened and there was no doubt Robert Peterson knew what Gabriel longed to know. The tone in the tall, gangly man's voice made it clear that he was indeed upset by what he had read. The blush in his face, a face wrinkled beyond his actual years, made it even clearer that Robert Peterson was more than just a little upset over what the letter had revealed. The man was infuriated. In the haste of his decision a few months before, Gabriel had set into motion a matter that had disheveled the most powerful man he knew, the man whose fury, even when bridled, had provoked the beatings, the banishments, and even the deaths of more than a few of Gabriel's neighbors and peers.

"Go ahead. Take it. It's yours, ain't it?" Robert Peterson's voice was gruff with question and disapproval, as he shoved the envelope slightly up against Gabriel's cheek.

"Yes sir. It is."

Gabriel had spent the past few weeks with the idea of the letter's arrival running through his innermost thoughts. At night, he dreamed about what he wanted the letter to say and in the day, each day since he had begun his wait, Gabriel worried about what the realization of his dream might mean to him and his family. As he labored in the field each blistering hot day, he worried and he also pondered over how all the work he had performed for years, each evening after he left the field, had long been driven by his desire that one day such a letter would arrive and the contents would change his entire life. Maybe. Hopefully.

Still, as he reached to take the envelope, Gabriel placed all of his mental energy into the steadying of his hand, for it had immediately begun to shake at the mere sight of the envelope he had waited so long to receive. Now, staring at the outcome of his quantum leap of faith, he could barely contain himself. However, he did not want Robert Peterson to guess at his excitement, for that would surely lend to a drastic reaction, so Gabriel thought to himself as intensely as he could, "Don't be nervous. Don't be nervous. DON"T be nervous." On this day, in that moment, unfortunately both his heart and his hand were ahead of his mind and the twitch in his outstretched hand did not go unnoticed.

After reading the letter and demanding to see Gabriel right away, Robert Peterson had already assumed that the boy would arrive frightened and imagining himself in the worst of scenarios. The shaking of the boy's hand spoke starkly to the accuracy of his assumption. Gabriel had every reason to be afraid. The arrival of the letter automatically revealed activity on his part that surely could lead to a nigger's demise and the young man obviously had elected to put himself and those who loved him at grave risk when he did what he did to receive the piece of paper between them. Never before had any of the niggers done anything as brazen as this and once he saw what he interpreted as fear in Gabriel's manner and mood, Robert Peterson's curiosity overrode his anger. If he was honest with himself, he would have to admit that he was actually somewhat amused by Gabriel's anxiousness, for it spoke to an acknowledgement of authority. Even if Gabriel had been defiant and had gotten beyond himself, the lad was still humble enough, weak enough to be scared. Hardly anything pleased Robert Peterson more than knowing folks were weaker than him and afraid of his wrath.

When he spoke again, his tone was slightly less abrasive and the color in his cheeks and forehead had begun to drain, returning his face to its normal pale, nearly white tone.

"Oh now, calm down Gabriel. Geesh. I ain't fixing to kill you," he declared, adding a slight chuckle, as he continued. "But now tell me boy. What in the world were you thinking, doing such a thing? If I didn't know any better, I would think you was trying to provoke me Gabriel. You trying to get a rise out of me son?"

Gabriel restrained display of the fury he felt from the reference to him as an offspring. The mean son of a bitch standing before him had the power and the right to say whatever he wanted, do whatever he wanted, including refer to him as "son" and such was a reality that infuriated Gabriel through and through. If he could have done so without endangering the lives of so many others, he would have taken the opportunity to strike the evil old man down with his bare hands right then and there, but life had taught Gabriel that opportunity seldom bore any outcomes in the lives of colored people. All things considered, there were no satisfactory options as to how to react and respond to Robert Peterson in a way that would also safeguard him and his family. Keeping his well-being and the best interests of his parents and his uncle in mind, Gabriel took a deep breath, lifted his eyes to meet squarely with those of the man who controlled his family's entire fate and, with as much humility in his voice as he could muster, offered what he hoped to be an acceptable explanation.

"I didn't mean to offend anyone, Sir. I got wind of it from one of my books and sent in for it. I just wanted to see if I could get it, Sir. My curiosity got the best of me, I suppose. I regret any offense to you, Sir. I was just reading it and saw that the paper said to fill it out and so I did. I didn't mean any harm by it, Sir. I assure you of that."

"Reading one of them doggone books Ms. Martha gave you, I reckon," Robert Peterson huffed.

"You know, Gabriel. This kind of foolishness is the very reason why I got a right mind to stop her from giving y'all niggers books and teaching y'all lessons y'all don't need anyhow," Robert Peterson scoffed, while slightly rocking back and forth on his feet. "Yeah. You going and doing something this ungrateful and downright dis-respectful tells me I just might need to close that so-called school of Ms. Martha's down and make them little niggers get on over into the field where I need 'em anyway. Nobody's too young to work and all that schooling ain't nothing but a waste of time. You go and do some-thing like this and it tells me maybe I just been way too lenient with this whole school thing, huh, son? What you think? Think I done got too soft-hearted toward my niggers?"

Gabriel knew he had to choose his words carefully. He knew the question was a trap. If he said no, then Robert Peterson would declare him to be ungrateful and close the school. The last thing Gabriel wanted was for anybody to suffer because of his ambitions and he certainly didn't want the children living in the Quarters to be pushed out to the fields even sooner than they were already. The thought of any child being denied the chance to learn to read and write on account of his own selfish endeavors pained Gabriel to the core. Before Robert Peterson could answer for him, he choked back his pride, swallowed his dignity and replied., slowly and very deliberately.

"Sir, all I know is that we appreciate every single thing you do for us. The schooling you allow teaches us discipline, Sir. And I know that I am a better worker for it. I believe the rest of the children are too, Sir. Yes Sir, it's been less runaways and more hard workers since you made us all go to school first. And I promise you, I won't get out of myself again. No Sir, you won't have nothing but hard work and appreciation from me from now on. This here, what I've gone and done was just silly, Sir, and I know you got to whip me. I deserve it Sir."

"So you ain't planning to do nothing about this letter?'

"No, Sir. I got my Ma and Pa and my uncle counting on me and I don't want to let them down. We aim to work ourselves out of what

8

we owe to you, Mr. Robert. I got to be here to do that and I wouldn't want to be nowhere but with my folks, anyhow, Sir."

By this time Robert Peterson had lit a pipe and tucked it in the corner of his mouth. Pulling on both suspenders with his thumbs and swaying back and forth on his black, hard-bottomed shoes, the big-bellied, skinny-legged man, with taut reddish skin and squinty eyes, shook his head and began to speak again, this time with an air of amusement in his voice.

"Well now that's what I figured Gabriel! I know you a smart nigger. I even brag on you myself sometimes. But now you and I both know that I can't be allowing one of my niggers to take on such a notion as this. I am an upstanding citizen, Gabriel. Many folk around here look up to me. My reputation is what makes this place as prosperous a business as it is. And I'm good to y'all niggers. Y'all don't never settle up with me for the housing and the food and the clothes, he said continuing to shake his head. "Every harvest season, I find y'all done ate and slept more than you produced and, still, I don't hardly ever turn any of you out."

Gabriel nodded his head in agreement as the loud and arrogant creature standing just a breath away began to speak with more animation and much more indignantly.

"So now, you tell me I have your word that nothing is going to come of this and I will forget it ever happened. You give me your word that you are going to stay put and keep me from having to really consider just how much your folks owe me, which I am pretty sure is way more than the three of them could ever pay off. If I ever have to consider such a thing, surely there would be no reason for me to keep those decrepit niggers around. So you tell me now that you are going to be around to work for the sake of the whole family and I'll forget all about this nonsense. Do I have your word, Gabriel?"

In a voice raised barely above a whisper Gabriel replied. "Yes, Sir, Mr. Robert. You have my word."

"Good!" Giggling and nodding in approval at Gabriel's declaration, Robert Peterson decided he had spent enough time warning the lad with his words and that the time had come to wrap up their little visit.

"Then I ain't going to even whip you Gabriel. I'm feeling right pleasant having your word and all. No, son. I don't think I'm in the mood to have you beat you today. You get back on down to the Quarters and enjoy your afternoon. No telling when the crops will allow us to have another one off, you know."

"Yes, Sir. And thank you, Sir. Thank you, kindly."

"You're welcome. And while you are feeling thankful, Gabriel, be sure to stop by Eli's and thank him personally for fetching you to come up here." Don't forget, you hear?"

"Yes, Sir. I'll be sure to do just that."

"You can go now."

As soon as Gabriel walked beyond the eyesight of anyone in or around the Peterson's mansion, he pulled the letter out of the inside of his shirt, where he had tucked it as he walked down the long hallway and headed out the servant's door. Now, a few feet off the pathway between the mansion and the fields that served as the front yard to the quarters, Gabriel sat in the tall grass and read the letter. As he unfolded the single sheet of paper, he felt as if his heart would burst out of his chest when he read the first sentence. "Dear Gabriel Loveman, The Board of Admissions for Garth Jordan College of Science and Engineering is pleased to announce the acceptance of your application for admission and your award of an academic scholarship......"

Chapter Two

GLEE AND GLOOM

S itting there reading his college acceptance letter word for word, Gabriel first felt a rush of joy and the sensation was incredible. He had done it. He had studied and learned and earned his way into the most prestigious institution of higher learning for people of color in the entire nation and he had even been granted free tuition. The letter was confirmation that everything he thought about himself and everything others believed about him from the day he was born was indeed true–that he was special, chosen and destined for greatness. His second read of the letter, though, drew him out of his initial glee, as the reality of the partial monetary award struck a nerve. His family had absolutely no money, none at all. Food, clothes and the tiny cabin where they slept was paid for every day by their labor in Robert Peterson's fields and financially, they lived life in the upside down position with regard to money matters. They all lived life knowing, with little doubt, Robert Peterson's bookkeeping was certain to ensure that such would be the case until their dying days. They worked for the sake of a meager existence and for the sole purpose of the Peterson Plantation's profit margin. The harsh reality was his family did not have a way to pay for their most basic needs. He could not imagine he would ever be able to come up with the money he would need to house, feed and clothe himself away home. By the third time Gabriel read the letter he had waited so long to receive, he was overwhelmed by the gravity of the implications and the thoughts his acceptance into college must have triggered in the mind of the wicked man who had placed the announcement in his hands. And suddenly, Gabriel understood exactly why Robert Peterson had instructed him to thank Eli "right away" for fetching him up to the main house.

As he ran past the raggedy shack he called home and over toward his neighbor's yard, Gabriel's heart sank at the sight of his elderly neighbor and friend. Eli, a gangly, tall but incredibly small-framed man, sitting on his own porch, hunched over, breathing deeply, drenched from head to toe in sweat and blood.

"Eli, what happened?"

"Well, I gotta beg yo' pardon, Gabriel. I ain't get to wait on yo' folks. Ole' Mistah Robert sent the field boss after me. I reckon I didn't run fast enough, didn't get you up there as directly as Mistah Robert wanted me to. So ole' Eli had to spend some of his day off with the whip."

"I'm so sorry, Sir. So sorry. I…"

Abruptly interrupting Gabriel, Eli lifted his head as he began to speak, his voice gruff with anguish and frustration, for any and every inch of any movement sent a seething jolt of pain up and down his spine and throughout his entire body. He closed his eyes and winced, as he confronted his young neighbor.

"Son!" Eli exclaimed, as he gasped for breath. "Don't you never ever say you sorry for a white man's evil deed. He do what he want to, when he want to do it! These here ain't the worse lashing I done been privy to. I 'clare, though. I do pray it be the very last of 'em. Good Lawd gone see fit to come and fetch ole' Eli soon enough."

The very thought seemed to relax Eli's body and he lowered both his head and his voice and almost managed a chuckle, as he struggled to finish.

"I'll be smiling even harder when He swoop me up into His lovin' arms if I know that Gabriel Loveman ain't come to no harm and ain't lose no pride, on account of me. So just help a ole' man in his house and don't say not nothin' else bout you being sorry for this day's lashing. Else you likely to take that smile right off of my dying face."

Any other young man standing before such a sight, hearing such a declaration would have been driven to sorrow and tears. And though Gabriel's chest swelled with regret and humility at the thought of the old man enduring such a horrible act simply due to his being in earshot distance when Robert Peterson read the letter and though Gabriel's heart was indeed heavy with guilt and sadness, he could not bring himself to shed a single tear. As a matter of fact, his eyes did not even water. Rather, they became fixed and focused on the reality before him and as he reached to lift Eli, his own plight became painfully clearer and, as he helped the old man move inside, Gabriel was overtaken by a heavy sense of gloom and dread.

The attack on Eli wasn't the first time Gabriel had encountered Robert Peterson's treachery. Treacherous acts were frequent occurrences on the Peterson Plantation. Lakes and rivers could be filled with the tears shed on an almost daily basis due to some horrible encounter or another by the people who Gabriel called family, neighbors and friends. Beatings, rapings, lashings and, not to mention, the driving of the field laborers to exhaustion every single day of planting season were all common occurrences and many residents of the Quarters had died from the heat of the sun and from the toil of the field, alone. Experiencing misery and bearing witness to it was the norm on the Peterson Plantation.

Still, hardly anything was as miserable as the sight of seeing an elderly gentleman, hunched over in pain, wiping his own tears with his own tattered, blood-soaked shirt. If Gabriel could have, he would have cried with the old man, out of sympathy, out of guilt or, if nothing else, out of the deeply-rooted respected he felt for Eli, but tears were foreign to Gabriel Loveman. He had not shed any since early one morning years ago. The last time Gabriel Loveman had visibly cried, the unimaginable horror—even for the Peterson Plantation dwellers—had occurred. As far as he was concerned, nothing worse could happen and, thus, nothing could be, would ever be, worth the shedding of any tears.

After Gabriel helped Eli to his feet and into his tiny shack of a home, he dressed the poor man's wounds and laid him down, all the while doing his best to keep the mood light by encouraging his old friend to rest up in order to be ready for the next day's labor. As soon as Eli drifted off to sleep, Gabriel went back to his own cabin and just as he had imagined, his parents and Uncle were there waiting, waiting and worrying. Once he reassured them that everything was alright and that he had merely spent the afternoon looking after Eli who had suffered trouble with the field manager, once he saw that his family was no longer nervous over his whereabouts that afternoon, Gabriel headed out of the back of the cabin, down the grassy path to his favorite oak tree. Segregated from the rest of the plantation's grove, Gabriel's tree was hardly ever frequented by others, as most of the other trees were much closer to the Quarters, where they overlapped and intertwined with one another. Collectively, they created a cavern of a sort, keeping the cluster of ragged cabins cool and sheltered from the abrasive sun that hung over the Peterson Plantation three-fourths of every year. Gabriel's oak, however, stood alone, off to itself and had branches so old and so low to the ground they seemed to form a private, shady room, where one could hide away from the rest of the world. The base of the tree was his haven and the day's events had him anxious for his quiet place.

Gabriel needed to be alone. He wanted to think about the letter and what finally having the news meant in totality. Yet, as he sat down at the foot of his tree, resting his foot on a raised root branch, Gabriel could not shake his anger over the beating Eli had endured, nor could he escape the sound of Robert Peterson's voice and the last word the monster of a man had said to him that afternoon. Right after he had been dismissed, when the last of the hateful threats against his life and his family's lives had been made, Gabriel, as protocol required, had placed his hat on his head and slightly bowed toward his oppressor, before turning to walk away. He had just gotten a few feet down the hallway when he heard Robert Peterson loudly clear his throat and defiantly say his brother's name.

They both knew why the name was spoken and they both knew no other words were needed to express how serious Robert Peterson took the matter that now existed between them. By speaking his brother's name, Robert Peterson knew he was issuing the most fretful threat of all and Gabriel was instantly reminded on how swift threats on the Peterson Plantation could become a reality.

As happy as he had been to finally receive word from the University of his acceptance, Gabriel found himself facing a dilemma that made for a most melancholy evening. As he sat alone under his favorite tree, wondering what to do about his circumstances, Gabriel found himself yearning for the company of his big brother and could not help but reflect on the event that created the void that had intensified with the events of the day. He had spent the past few years avoiding any recollection of the worst happening of his life and, for the most part, he had done so successfully by focusing on his studies and the relentless work required of him as a field hand. Any remaining room for preoccupation was filled up by Gabriel's steadfast attention to his beloved girlfriend, Ella. Ironically, on this day, the day of the arrival of what should have been the best news of his life, he was on reprieve from the field, there was no lesson outstanding that he had not already mastered and any attention to Ella would have to include a discussion about his news, something he was not quite ready to share with his love. Still, he needed someone to talk to and how he wished he could have turned to the brother who would have known exactly what to say to help him make sense of his entire situation.

Quite a bit of time had passed since Gabriel had allowed himself to think about Benjamin. Even if Robert Peterson hadn't spoken his name, receiving the letter would have eventually brought thoughts of his big brother to mind. The letter, or rather the contents of the letter, had long been a prediction of Benjamin Loveman. Like Gabriel, he had spent years with the notion at the forefront of his mind, looking forward to the day the invitation would land in the hands of his little brother. Unlike Gabriel, Benjamin had never doubted that one day such a letter would arrive, take effect and be the modem for his little brother's entrance into a world more accepting of a black genius. Now holding the letter in hand, Gabriel was struck by the stark reality of not being able to share the letter with the person who had more faith in him than he had in himself. Sitting under the tree, letter in hand, hat on his lap, Gabriel for the first time in a long time, acknowledged the absence of Benjamin from his world. He had no choice but to do so, for if he could have, right away, he would have given the letter to his big brother, who surely would have been standing beside him, grinning from ear to ear with pride and anxiously waiting to read the words of the letter for himself. But there were no other hands to hold the letter, no sibling to stand behind him as he took the news all in, no big brother to see beaming with pride and no Benjamin, smiling and singing with glee at the proof of his baby brother's brilliance.

The letter, along with Robert Peterson's reaction and Eli's misfortune, had conjured up thoughts Gabriel had refused to think for years, thoughts that were certain to overwhelm any decision on his part to move forward in his life. Unbearable thoughts they were, indeed, but in the late afternoon, in the early evening of the day Gabriel had most looked forward to for so long, he found himself thinking of the day, the night, rather, that he wished he could forget forever. For a long time, Gabriel had found a way to push the thoughts of that terrible night so far to the back of his memory that any observer could be easily convinced that he actually had forgotten the matter. As far as his family, friends, and neighbors knew, since the moments after he was first made aware of what happened to his brother, Gabriel had never spoken of and never cried over Benjamin's death. Five long years had gone by and though he still could not bring himself to shed tears, on this day, the day that should have been the best day of his life, Gabriel could not help but to think back to the night everything changed. Sitting there under his favorite oak, with his acceptance letter in his hands, Gabriel found himself with ample time to need and miss his brother and to reminisce about the evil act that had taken Benjamin away from him forever.

Chapter Three

LYING AND LYNCHING

That night was just the kind of night that would bring trouble and sorrow. The air was bitter cold and a thick dampness burdened what little was left of the late summer breeze. Everything was still and the eerie quietness was interrupted only every now and again by the screech of an owl. The bird's hollow, piercing squawk was loud, sharp and seemed to serve as an announcement of the tragedy yet to come. For at least an hour or so, no one inside the Loveman cabin had said a word. Instead, everyone sat quietly and preoccupied themselves with an occupation that might as well not have existed, for each mind was heavily weighed with worry. Rosalee Loveman looked to be darning the same sock for the fifth time, when she really was reciting the Lord's prayer over and over, silently to herself. John Loveman was finishing his nightly Bible reading. The page detailing the perils of Job was nothing but a mere blur. Still, he stared for fear that if he lifted his eyes from the Book, his swollen heart would burst and he would not be able to hold back his tears. David Loveman, a man known to avoid pretentiousness at all cost, simply sat in the wicker chair, rocking back and forth, wringing his hands until they were just about chapped and raw. No doubt he imagined the worst of scenarios. Some twenty years or so before, he himself had barely escaped a similar plight as the one

19

feared Benjamin might be facing and so he sat feeling more helpless than ever, waiting for the return of the nephew he loved as if he were his own child. Gabriel, the youngest member of the Loveman clan and the most anxious of all, sat halfway sprawled across the kitchen table, surrounded by books and work tablets, trying desperately to focus on his preparation for the next day's school session. A usual quick study, his anxiety for his big brother's arrival home disrupted his focus and he could not concentrate. The queasiness he felt deep in the bottom of his chest overwhelmed his attention span and so, while the books were placed in front of him, he had captured little to nothing of what they had to offer him, on this haunting evening.

For all the same reasons and then for unique and very special reasons, every member of the Loveman family longed for the exact same event. They all wanted the front door to swing open with just a little too much force, just as it had each night before, bearing Benjamin's entrance to their humble abode and closing out of his long workday. They all wanted to hear the beginning of a sweet love song or a soothing church hymn in the voice of a most glorious tenor, perfect in pitch, that carried over and across the fields of the plantation and down the path to their small cabin, into the ears of his loving family members, who all relied on a nightly song for their awareness of his whereabouts. If nothing else, the Loveman family wanted to see the hazy glimmer of a swinging lantern that could always be seen from the tiny window overlooking their front porch. The light always seemed to shine brighter and brighter as Benjamin made his way closer and closer to the home where he belonged, the cabin where his loving family sat night after night awaiting his arrival. That night each family member looked desperately for the light that many nights had brought the most welcome relief when the dark had arrived, the singing had stopped, but the door had yet to swing open- the light, the lantern, that lit up the night just as the one they awaited lit up their heart and souls. This wanting, this wait was a routine the Lovemans endured night after night during the planting season, an endurance that mostly went unmentioned, for such was the tradeoff for Benjamin's love.

As gut wrenching and nerve-wracking as the wait always was, that night was the worst ever. Perhaps their fright was due to the stillness of the wind. Perhaps the heaviness of the air that was particularly cold and harsh for a late summer's eve made them all the more uneasy. Perhaps it was the continuous screeching of the owl. Perhaps, just perhaps, more than anything else, their fears were rooted in the fact that never before had there been this long a time between the song ending, the light shining brightly and the door swinging open. After the second hour passed, Father did as fathers in his situation were trained to do. As he closed his Bible, John Loveman looked at his wife, whose head was hung so heavy with fear and worry that she could not return his gaze.

"I will go and get him and bring him home. I promise," he said, gently.

In a very bare whisper, Rosalee Loveman responded. "Twenty years, John Loveman, and you ain't never made a promise to me you couldn't keep. Don't start now. You go," she whispered, as she tilted her head to the side, tears streaming down past her chin, falling, one after the other onto the sock that lay in her lap. "I'll stay here. I'll sit here and pray for him and for you and I'll wait here, right here in this chair, until you come home."

∞

Early the next morning, sometime right after sunrise, he entered the back door, alone. His shirt and pants were covered in mud. His hands and his face were covered with ashes and dirt. There had been a burial.

As his wife sobbed uncontrollably and as his youngest son lie shaking on the floor of the cabin, John told of how he found Benjamin hours before and how he buried a body unfit to be seen, even by the closest of kin. Without emotion and without the shed of a single tear, he told his family that their beloved Benjamin was gone away from them forever. What he did not tell them, what he could not bring himself to repeat were the grimsly details of his discovery. John could not tell them that, after he happened upon the lantern, which was still burning, lighting the area where his oldest boy last prayed, sang and toiled the land with his precious hands, he had walked for almost an hour looking for Benjamin. Seeing the lantern burning brightly in the spot where his son should have been had furthered the grim suspicion that had been lingering in John's mind since long before he had left their cabin. And so, with a heavy heart and troubled mind, he began to search for his beloved boy who had grown to be such a wonderful man. With each step that led John deeper and deeper into the thick of the woods surrounding the Peterson Plantation, the faint hope of finding his dear boy alive withered. When he first noticed the stench of smoke and burning flesh, John almost turned and ran. Only the thought of wild animals destroying what was left of his child kept him from turning back, that image and the idea of children possibly coming across the body during what was supposed to be a time of play and frolic. Neither instance was unheard of but rather was as common as the matter before him. Besides, John knew that if he could not bring Benjamin home to his mother, he would at least have to give the woman the right of knowing her son had been properly laid to rest. As painful as never seeing Benjamin again would be for her, John knew Rosalee would want to know that Benjamin had been found. For the sake of her sanity, John would have to be able to tell his wife that Benjamin's body had been buried and that a prayer had been offered for his dear and departed soul.

For as long as he could remember, John had joined in the search for sons of relatives and friends who often found them in the worst of plights. He had seen grown men cry and vomit at the sight of their boys swinging from trees or lying headless and castrated in shallow, muddy waters. He had even seen the body of a little girl ravished and then beaten to death. Before the poor child could be discovered by loved ones and friends, mosquitoes and other wild insects had diminished her body to mere fragments of flesh and mostly bare bones. Still nothing John had ever seen, witnessed or heard before could have prepared him for that night's wretched discovery.

As he cut Benjamin's charred body from the rope, John did not cry. As he struggled to keep some of the flesh on his son's face and torso intact, he did not cry. Even when he plugged the slit in the throat that carried the most musical of voices, he held back his tears, but when he lifted his dead son's arms and saw that his hands had been severed and when he realized that such had more than likely occurred when his boy was still alive and breathing, John shivered and cried. First he found the hands, the hands that had never brought pain to another human being or even to a creature, the hands that cared so tenderly for each person or thing they touched, the huge hands that carried a Mother for whatever distance, long or short, if she barely suggested she was tired, the skilled hands that completed the chores of a sick uncle and then prepared that Uncle's bath and then bathed that Uncle until he was clean and rested, the same sturdy hands that had tossed a little brother into the air in play and jest well beyond the age and size when such was easy to do- gifted hands that belonged to the most beautiful man, inside and out, and to a man that had never lifted those hands to harm anyone or anything, even though they were the strongest of hands. What was left of Benjamin's hands was nothing more than fragments of bloodied flesh and bones. Still, John held them as closely as he could to his cracked and weary heart. As he wept, he decided right then and there that he would be the only member of what was left of his family to bear that night's horror, entirely. He had to tell them Benjamin was dead and they would know that he was hung but, as he sat alone in the woods surrounded by his son's tattered remains, John decided his loved ones would never know just how far the killers had gone to destroy Benjamin's beautiful body.

With each tear he shed, John became more and more determined to keep the gruesome details of the lynching all to himself for the rest of his life.

As he sat alone in the dark woods, holding what was left of his boy, John's cry was the cry of a man who lived hoping against hope that this awfulness would never happen to him.

"Black boys die young."

That was the declaration made to John by his own father moments right after Benjamin's birth and his father's dismal advice rang in his ears as he rocked the lifeless body of his firstborn. As the prediction manifested and became John's reality, as he cuddled the remains of his oldest son, Benjamin James Loveman, John could hear his father's instruction in the back of his mind, in the background of his own wailing cry.

"Love him and cherish him. Teach him good each day of his life, which will probably be a very short one."

Why white men lynched black boys was the unanswered and lingering question of the old. Benjamin's killers had long stated their hatred for the singing nigger who year after year produced the season's best crops. Benjamin had been warned many times by them that his days were numbered. Their bitterly made threats were serious, defined and frequent. They were not idle and no one took them lightly, for the taking of a black man's life for any given reasons was the birthright of a white man in the South. The four men who participated in Benjamin's death that night had all at one time or another reminded him of his worthlessness, despite his talents and his good nature. Their intentions had been spoken aloud and on more than a few occasions he had been approached by them, sometimes as a group, sometimes individually, and forewarned that his days on earth were numbered and that, at a time of their choosing, he would meet with a horrid fate. Each family member and every neighbor and friend, on one occasion or another, had begged Benjamin to not farm alone at night, to not provide those who so unreasonably yet so resoundingly hated him with the easy opportunity for his capture and attack. Benjamin's response was always the same.

"If they are going to kill me, then nothing, no place, and no one can keep them from it. Let them find me where I belong, doing what I was born to do. At least they will remember that when they came for me, I was farming. My death won't change the fact that I am a man with a gift from the good Lord above. They will find me and take me from what I love, farming this here land."

And so they did. They found him, ran him into the woods where they beat him, stabbed him, chopped of both his hands and slit his throat before hanging his body and setting him ablaze. They watched him burn until they could stomach the ghastly, grotesque sight and stench no more. Then they went home, kissed their wives lovingly on the cheek, ate their dinners and played with their own sons. The act of taking the life of a nigger in such a way was all in a day's work, a pastime for white men in the South and that night, each man in Benjamin Loveman's lynch mob slept soundly, without a conscious thought of the pain they had caused.

For the Loveman family, the pain was immeasurable, beyond description. And so, for the most part, after the morning after the worst night of their lives, after John had explained that he could not bring Benjamin home, after he picked his youngest and now only living son up from the floor and after he had moved his weeping wife from the tiny kitchen to the bed that became her haven for the next few days after she had learned of her eldest child's fate- after his brother, David, had prayed and begged God out loud to have mercy on their family and upon his befallen nephew's soul and to curse the lives of the ones with the blood on their hands- after all that occurred that miserable morning after the worst night ever, the Loveman family did not speak to one another or to anyone else about the lynching of Benjamin Loveman.

Unlike the Lovemans, their neighbors, both black and white, far and near, often spoke about what happened to the handsome, farmer, who was known for his singing and for his ability to produce the most vibrant, plentiful crops. Black folks spoke about how inevitable the murder was and, yet, how the actual occurrence was still a shock and incredibly saddening for all who knew him. White folks spoke about how inevitable the unfortunate incident was considering the brazen and arrogant character of the hard-headed, nigger, who, as far as they were concerned, finally got what was coming to him. However, white folks who would never participate in a lynching but who also would never take a stand in protest whispered amongst themselves utterances of shame and embarrassment that such an evil act was considered common recreation. Secretly, their hearts went out to the Loveman family and silently, they prayed for Benjamin's soul. Little did they know that they were the white people the Lovemans had to pray the hardest not to hate. They were the very people who had the power to stop the lynchings and the treacherous murders of negroes for the silliest of reasons and oftentimes for no reason at all, except such was allowed. Yet death after terrible death, they only preached their protest to those who shared their sentiment and never did they say to any member of any lynch mob "you are wrong to kill and the life you take is that of a human being." To the Lovemans they were just as much a part of the mob as the ones who actually partook in what was clearly killings but not crimes by their society's standard. Indeed, whether you were a grieving loved one, one of the killers that caused the grief or whether you were the silent detester of the senseless acts, the ultimate consensus was all the same. Black boys in the South stood to die young. And Benjamin died at eighteen.

Chapter Four

PASSION AND PATIENCE

Sitting there reminiscing on the worst night of his life, Gabriel had been so consumed by his reflection of his brother's death, he hadn't realized Ella had come looking for him and was sitting beside him, questioning him about what had him so preoccupied. Though she was hardly ever put off by his aloofness, something about Gabriel's mood that evening was different and whatever he was thinking about had kept him from noticing her presence and Gabriel always noticed her. Without knowing why, Ella felt disturbed, nervous and by the time Gabriel realized she was sitting there, talking to him, her voice was filled with panic.

"Do you hear me talking to you? Gabriel! Gabriel Lovemman, I know you hear me." Once again Gabriel had drifted away, gone to some place in his mind where no one could reach him. Ella was accustomed to his tendency to let his mind wander but for him to do so now when they were finally had a chance to share a few intimate moments was upsetting and Gabriel could hear her frustration in her voice as she quizzed him.

"What are you thinking about?" The accusatory tone in Ella's voice snapped Gabriel out of his deep thought and suddenly he realized she had been sitting alongside him for more than a few minutes.

Her impatience was quite noticeable, as she continued to prod him with her anxious inquiry.

"If you got your mind on some other gal, Gabriel Loveman, you just go ahead and tell me now. Ain't no need for you to be wasting your time with little, simple-minded Ella when you can have anybody you want. I'm sitting right here and your mind is clearly on something else, or someone else, I suppose!" Ella exclaimed.

No matter how worried he was about the possible outcomes of the letter and regardless of how forlorn he felt from reminiscing over his belated brother, Gabriel did not want Ella to have a moment of concern regarding the way he felt for her. No situation, nor any sadness could ever compromise how he felt about her. More than anything else, he aimed to always love and protect her. He hated seeing her upset and when he spoke, he did so to reassure her and to calm her down.

"No, no, no. Baby, I'm sorry. I wasn't thinking about no other girl. I was just thinking that I don't need to get you in trouble. I was thinking that you are a good girl, the best a man could ask for and I don't need to be sitting here getting us into any kind of fix, knowing we ain't married. There is absolutely nobody else on my mind but you, never has been and never will be. And don't call yourself names. You know I don't like that. We both know there is not one single thing simple about that mind of yours. No, that brain of yours is always working and right now your thoughts have worked you right up into a fit."

Gabriel paused long enough to pull Ella closer to him. He wanted her to feel his sincerity and he also knew he needed them both to move out from under the tree. He meant every word he had just spoken and suddenly he was keenly aware of their physical attraction. Being alone with her was a rarity and in the past few months, he had found himself yearning to be with her, more and more. His desire was outmatched only by his respect and concern for her well-being, as he had long been determined to always handle her with deliberate caution and care. To say the least, she was precious to him and Gabriel wanted her to always know Ella would cherish and protect her.

"I tell you what, let's get up from here and go for a walk through the peach tree grove. I'll pick you some real pretty peaches."

" I guess that is your way of telling me that you'd rather have a peach pie than have me while we are sitting under this here tree."

"Now that is where you are wrong. I'm just going to settle for that pie. That's the best I can do for the sweetest, prettiest girl in the world." Gabriel whispered in Ella's ear as he pulled her up to her feet and snuggled her in his arms.

"You are charming, Mr. Loveman. If nothing else, you are most charming."

"You forgot handsome and brilliant!" Gabriel said with a hearty laugh.

"Well you ain't that handsome," Ella chuckled, as she replied. "But everybody knows how brilliant your are. And I know, Gabriel." she said, her voice growing serious in tone. With a hint of resignation, she brought their close call with passion to an end. "And I know that the trouble you don't want to get me in is in the same kind of trouble that will get in the way of what you can do now. Your brain can get you away from here and Lord knows if I can't get out of here myself, I will at least have the comfort of loving the one who does make it out. So come on. Let's head on over to that big peachtree right in the middle of the grove. I know the peaches on it are just ripe for the picking and sweet enough for the pie."

As the two of them walked hand-in-hand, making their way over to the fruit trees near the Quarters, the sun began to set and, for a few minutes, time seemed to stand still, as Gabriel relished in the love between the two of them. As much uncertainty as he felt since the arrival of the letter, he needed the moment they were sharing, needed the reassurance and the comfort their relationship brought to his life. He needed Ella, his friend, his confidant and his love more than ever before.

❦

Later on that evening, as Ella sat waiting on the pies to finish baking, her thoughts drifted back to the first time she ever saw the man she had come to love so. She had only been on the Peterson Plantation for a few days when she met Gabriel Loveman. She and her mother had come over from the farm where they had lived with her father until he dropped dead of a heart attack at the ripe old age of thirty-five. The landowner had given them three days to bury him and move out since there was no way she and her mother could keep up enough work to earn their stay. She was only a little girl but life had seemed to have forgotten her youth. Her father's death, though sad, had not been the most traumatic of events for the young Ella and she was known for being wise beyond her years. Life had taught her lessons very early on and few were the girls who had her grace and warmth. With all that she had been through, her sweet ways were somewhat of an enigma to those who knew that she had been molested and had watched as a playmate was beaten and drowned for stealing bread for an ailing grandmother.

By the time she arrived at the Peterson Plantation, hardly anything about life was alarming to Ella. She wasn't even alarmed by the welcome speech given by Mr. Robert Peterson, which consisted of a curt declaration that, as a demonstration of his charity, he was going to allow Ella and her mother to move in with her aunt, whose husband had also recently died. With an unforgettable smugness, he had reminded her mother to never forget that he was going above and beyond what he usually did for niggers in her circumstance and that out of the goodness of his heart, he was even allowing Ella to go to school, so long as Ella, her mother and aunt all kept to themselves and kept quiet about his graciousness. Right before her eyes, he emphasized his warning and control over their lives by sexually molesting Ella's mother. First, he peeked around to make sure his wife was still preoccupied with her typical afternoon exercise of bird watching and whiskey sipping and then, with the most wicked smirk on his face, he pulled Ella's mother to his side and harshly groped her breasts, as he chuckled and commented about how amused he was by the lightness of her child's skin tone. Ella would never forget the look of fright on her mother's face when he stopped and reached his hand out in her direction or the relief they both felt when he halted because his wife had hurriedly darted into the room to exclaim her excitement at the sighting of a blackbird.

Throughout the horrible introduction to the Peterson Plantation, Ella never flinched. As upsetting as the whole scene should have been to the little girl, Ella wasn't rattled, nor was she taken aback by the tiny shack her aunt lived in or by the fact that she and her mother would have to share a small bed. She was not unnerved by the long hours her mother and aunt worked everyday for no pay and she wasn't noticeably disturbed by how the other girls in the Quarters pretty much gave her the silent treatment on sight simply because she was cursed with what most of them called "good hair" and fair skin. What threw her off guard, what finally shook her world and what took Ella totally aback was her first encounter with Gabriel Loveman.

Ella had just had a heated exchange with one of the girls who had decided that the new girl thought she was better than everyone else because of her light complexion and long black ponytail. She was flustered and tired, and for the first time since her father's death, she found herself near tears. With the ease of a gazelle, Gabriel had walked up to her and in the most gentle yet sturdy voice counseled her.

"Don't let them see you cry. Unless you want them to keep on you making you cry."

Gabriel then took her books and placed them on what he obviously decided what would be her classroom seat, which was right next to his. They didn't say much else that day. As a matter of fact, long and involved conversation between them was the unusual occurrence and still not the norm. From the moment they met, in some mystical, inexplicable way, Gabriel and Ella were always in communication with one another and their friendship deepened rapidly. Over a period of time, all the other students, even the girls who first hated her, began to accept her and treat her with the same respect and care they had always bestowed upon Gabriel. The general consensus seemed to be that if Gabriel Loveman thought it best to accept this strange girl with quiet, matronly ways, then so should they, since they all believed Gabriel to be the smartest person they knew, one who always seemed to know the right thing to do. Though his manner was rather reserved, there was a certain trustworthy strength in his carriage that made his judgment reliable as far as others were concerned and so they adopted his acceptance of Ella and followed his lead by respecting her unusual ways and admiring her peculiar physical traits.

Gabriel's peers would never have imagined just how weak at heart he sometimes felt, especially since Benjamin's death and now even more, since he received the acceptance letter. Although many considered his quietness as a sign of his coming of age, most still were puzzled that Gabriel hardly spoke about his future plans and at how he hardly ever talked about his brother Benjamin, how he carried on as if his brother had never existed at all, and, thus, was never lynched. Hardly anyone could understand his reaction to Benjamin's death, given the obvious closeness of the two siblings and Gabriel's well-known admiration for his older brother. They wondered how he could he carry on so quietly, so calmly, as if nothing terrible had actually happened to his brother and how could he be so guarded about the possibility of leaving the Peterson Plantation for a better life somewhere else. To them, Gabriel's desire to leave should have been compounded by his brother's death and everyone who knew and cared for him expected him to announce his confidence in his brilliance and his reliance upon his academic abilities to make the way for him to leave and never come back. Yet, as the years passed and he remained more quiet about his future, those around him understood Gabriel less and less.

Without much explanation from him, Ella understood Gabriel's way, his manner. She had the unfortunate but sound wisdom of those who developed secret sorrows early on in life. Ella knew that Gabriel was struggling with the guilt of leaving and the misery of staying. She wanted him to stay and she was hopeful that he would leave. Her desire for him to remain was based on her own selfish needs and her earnest love for him. Her hope that he would go was rooted in her appreciation of his genius and, of course, her unconditional love for him. And so in Ella, Gabriel found a soulmate, a confidant and nurturer and an ardent supporter of anything he decided to do.

Chapter Five

FEAR AND FAMILY

As proud as he was to receive the letter, as happy as he was to know that people somewhere well beyond Chester County considered him intelligent enough for acceptance into the world of academics and higher learning, Gabriel knew he could not mention the contents of the letter to his family. The letter that liberated him on one hand burdened him on the other and Gabriel knew that burden would extend to the ones who loved him. The University had deemed him worthy of a scholarship that would cover all of the costs associated with his tuition, books, and academic fees, but his application had arrived too late for the waiver of the fees for his room and board, at least such would be the case for his first year of enrollment. He couldn't even begin to imagine leaving without also having to consider the plight of his family and how unlikely they would be able to sustain themselves if he were to actually act on the letter. Even if he wasn't facing a probable death if Robert Peterson so much as caught wind of any notion on his part to take the school's offer seriously, Gabriel still would be facing the reality of his financial dilemma. Room and board was estimated at an incredible amount of one hundred dollars for each semester and though Gabriel could work at night and on the weekends to earn the money needed for the second semester, he had no way to pay for the first few months of his relocation. While he knew in his heart that just about everyone in the Quarters, young and old, alike, would contribute any extra money they had to help him go off to school, there were two other things to consider. One certainty was a clear and painful reality for all those Gabriel knew and loved and that not a single one of them hardly had any such thing as extra money. The other undeniable truth was that getting the word out to garner any help from friends and neighbors would heighten the risk of Robert Peterson finding out Gabriel intended to leave. The slightest risk in that regard could result in the suffering of horrific consequences for him and anyone who tried to assist him.

Gabriel knew that sharing the news of his acceptance with his parents and his Uncle David, telling them about it, even as a casual mention, would either plague them with guilt or give them the cruel hope that he may actually be the first Loveman to leave the Peterson Plantation, if by some miracle, he avoided the wrath of Robert Peterson and found a way to pay for his room and board. Folks in the Quarters believed in God, but miracles were beyond their imagination, and Gabriel was no exception. He was faithful to the extent that he had no problem accepting and experiencing God's love and control over his life, but his faith was heavily compromised by the harsh realities of plantation life and the tragic loss of his older brother. He only expected God to be there and see him through. His expectation of miracles and his willingness to take incredible leaps of faith seemed to have passed away with Benjamin and any remnants of such were as faint and fleeting as his happy memories of life before the lynching. As much as he wanted to tell his family about the letter and as much as he hated to keep the matter a secret, he knew he had no choice. Telling his Mother, Father and dear uncle was simply not an option. And just as much as he knew they could never know about his acceptance unless and until he made his final decision, Gabriel knew that there were two people he had to tell.

Ella, his sweetheart, would have to be told. From the moment she knew his application had actually been submitted, she had become just as anxious for the response, maybe even more. She wanted the good news she was sure the letter would bring because she believed in Gabriel more than anyone, except the only other person with whom Gabriel would have shared the news, if only he were still alive. With Benjamin gone, Ella was now the closest person to Gabriel and she knew just about everything there was to know about him. She was his most trusted confidant and the object of his affection, his love in the truest sense of the word and the one person on the Peterson Plantation who actually believed in miracles. Although he was anxious at the thought of saying or doing anything that stood to upset or trouble her, Gabriel could not keep anything from Ella, especially something as precious, complicated and confusing as his acceptance to the University.

There was another person who deserved to know the news of the letter because she was the very person who had insisted that he apply. Actually, she had mailed the application on his behalf. She had spent the last thirteen years or so doing all she could to assist him, or better stated, to service him, for his brilliance was in little need of help. Still, she had made guiding, educating and encouraging Gabriel her life's mission. She was his teacher, his mentor and a close and dear friend.

∞

Walking down the pathway to the school where he had spent so many days and, in recent years, so many evenings, Gabriel thought back to the very first time he had ever taken such a walk, the very first day he entered the door of the makeshift school and met the woman who would change his life forever.

"Come in. You must be Gabriel. I've got a seat for you right up here on the front row."

The voice addressing the five year old Gabriel was the softest and the sweetest he ever heard. As he lifted his head to reply, his breath was cut short by her astonishing beauty, a beauty that had nothing to do with the color of her skin. Even at the mere age of five, Gabriel was old enough to know that some folks most often and much too graciously assigned beauty and class to almost every white woman they encountered. Somehow, though, even in his youthfulness, Gabriel knew that Ms. Martha's beauty had nothing to do with the whiteness of her skin and that she was the beholder of the kind of beauty that transcended age, race, size, and anything that made people distinctive. She was lovely, in the purest and most universal kind of way, inside and out. Her deep and heartfelt compassion for the children of the Quarters and the poor white children who lived in Chester County governed her life's decisions and, instead of taking her place in society as the wife of a wealthy Southern plantation owner or instead of moving to a more populated and cultured area where she most assuredly would have blossomed, Martha had resigned herself to the life of a spinster, a teacher, with no husband and no children of her own. To her, even her loneliest moments were minimal compensation for the joy she felt anytime she was able to help a child of the South transcend beyond the limitations and boundaries set by the social ills of plantation life. She easily identified students who were exceptionally gifted and recognized an extraordinary mind almost immediately and every once in awhile, God would reward her dedication and sacrifice by allowing her to keep company with pure genius.

The day five-year old Gabriel Loveman walked through her door, Martha knew her life would never be the same. She had heard about him long before he arrived at her schoolhouse and within moments of their first encounter, she understood why everyone was so captivated the little boy wonder of the Quarters. Gabriel Loveman was extraordinary. Amazingly, before he could even walk, he was talking and speaking in full sentences. By the time Gabriel was three years old, everyone who knew him was aware that he was uniquely and extraordinarily gifted. Whatever he saw, whatever he heard, he remembered. The clarity of his recall and the little boy's ability to regurgitate just about any information that was given to him directly or that he overheard was mind-boggling. People throughout the Quarters would stop by the Loveman's cabin as often as possible just to marvel at the child who seemed to have a machine for a mind. Asking Gabriel questions or demanding that he relay some event or happening he had observed or heard about became a favorite pastime amongst his neighbors and for quite some time, Martha had heard tales of the little boy who could recant anything he heard once and instantly do anything he had been shown how to do one time. From the first day he stepped foot in her tiny schoolhouse, Gabriel Loveman swiftly became her star student.

∞

Gabriel headed down the pathway to the schoolhouse, a cabin three times the size of the others in the Quarters. A few years before, a wooden fence had been placed around the school with the hope of keeping small critters outside and the small children inside the play yard that ran along the front and sides of the building. With only one tiny tree and a few bushes for shade, the grass surrounding the school never grew too tall, nor did it ever turn as green as the other land on the estate. Rather, the foliage remained the same greenish-brown year round. Still, the children of the Quarters made no complaint. The play yard and their little school was sacred, safe ground, where they were free to learn, play and allowed to forego the hideous work activity that went on beyond the wooden fence. For years, Ms. Martha had not only provided an education to the children of the Quarters, she had also watched over the toddlers and the smaller ones who were not yet old enough to attend school. Why she did so remained a mystery to most, but the children and the parents, alike, loved her for her benevolence and commitment and, although she was white, she was considered by most to be a friendly neighbor within the Quarters community.

As Gabriel approached the school door, he saw Martha emerge from her hiding place, behind a bush at the corner of the pale yellow cabin and realized he was about to interrupt a very intense game of hide-and-seek between teacher and students. The children immediately ran toward her as they squealed delightfully over their capture.

As she slightly struggled to unravel herself from the small mob of miniature people gathered around her, she called out to her favorite student of all.

"Why Gabriel! What brings you here this afternoon?"

As usual, Gabriel's even-toned voice did not suggest his mood or the reason for his visit.

"I need to speak with you Ma'am."

Martha had known Gabriel long enough to know that although he was mostly a man of few words, when he did speak, whatever he said carried great meaning. He had been a serious child when she first met him. He then went on to become a serious student, who had morphed into the very serious young man standing before her. The look on his face was confusing, however, and Martha could not tell if he needed to discuss something sad or exciting. Right away, though, she was alarmed.

"You children run along home now. It's soon to be supper time and your parents will be looking for you."

As the children darted toward the gate to the play yard, they all shouted their cheerful goodbyes to the lady they had come to love so much. A few of them spoke to Gabriel, but most of them shot right past him with nothing more than a quick glance and a nod in his direction, though they all knew all about him. All of their lives they had heard about the boy genius who lived among them in the Quarters. Gabriel Loveman was the one they were supposed to grow up to be just like, if they parents had their way. For years, folks in the quarters spoke about how smart he was so much and with such pride and awe, he had become somewhat of a living legend among the youngsters of the Quarters. On this eve, though, Gabriel felt anything but legendary. He felt excited and validated but he also felt afraid, fearful in a way that was unfamiliar to him. When he was close enough for Martha to look into his eyes, she noticed his fretfulness right away and instantly her heartbeat began to quicken in pace.

"Is everything alright Gabriel? Nothing's happened has it?"

Martha knew that the environment she lived in was the backdrop for tragic news and someone coming to her school to bring her awful news of a death of a parent or one of her precious students was not nearly as unusual an occurrence as it should have been.

Gabriel could tell the extent of the worry in her question and quickly calmed her with his response.

"Oh, no M'aam, Ms. Martha, it's nothing like that. Nobody's dead…..at least not yet. I got the letter, is all."

"You did?" she exclaimed.

"Yes, I did."

As Gabriel reached inside his shirt and pulled out the envelope containing his acceptance letter, he decided to go ahead and share the rest of the news with her.

"Mr. Robert got it first. He opened it. He knows what it says."

"What did he say to you Gabriel? You didn't have any trouble did you?"

"Well, I didn't. He let me know right away, though, that my going would be more than trouble for me and my family, much more than trouble. To make sure I understood him, he had the manager beat poor old Eli.

"For what?!"

Martha was disgusted by the horrible acts the owner of the Peterson Plantation committed or had someone else commit against the very people who put all of his money in his pockets and whose labor was the driving force behind his wealth. He was a wicked man. Always had been and he and Martha both took every effort to avoid the crossing of one another's paths. Whenever she did see him, whenever the needs of the school or the children she taught and cared for so demanded, her visits and conversations with him were always as brief as possible. They both preferred it that way, although for very different reasons.

Slightly shrugging his shoulders, Gabriel answered her as best he could.

"For existing, I guess. For being at the wrong place at the wrong time, when the letter came and for having the misfortune of being the one to fetch me up to the main house to meet with Mr. Robert to get it. I guess mostly he beat that old man to let me know that worse, much worse would come to me if I try to leave."

Martha could tell that Gabriel had been shaken by the day's events. As she read the letter, he eased down into one of the tiny desks and Martha could not help but notice how much of a man he had become. He could barely squeeze his tall frame into the seat, taking up all the space between the chair and the attached desktop. Her mind flashed back to when he was so tiny that not only did he easily fit but there was a huge gap of space between his body and the desktop and when the long legs that now stretched out before him, dangled over the floor beneath his desk chair. As she looked down at the young, handsome man, she was overcome with emotion. The years, as troubling as they often had been, had flown by and she found herself on the verge of tears at the thought of what was soon to come.

"Is that what he told you?" she asked, quickly collecting herself and folding the letter, tucking it into the envelope, as she handed it back over to Gabriel.

"In so many words. Or in one word, should I say to be correct."

Gabriel placed the envelope back on the inside of his shirt. He decided right then and there that, except for when he slept, the letter would always be with him, hidden safely away and available to him anytime he wanted to read it.

As difficult as the conversation was to have, Martha had to know the exact details of Gabriel's last interaction with the owner of the plantation. She had to know what he was up against and so she pressed harder.

"What word was that, Gabriel? What EXACTLY did he say?"

Gabriel stood up and looked at his teacher, his friend, straight in her eyes and, with as much emotional constraint as he could muster, repeated to her what the most hateful man they knew had said to him after giving him the acceptance letter.

"He said….Benjamin."

With that, Gabriel turned and walked slowly out of the door and out of the school yard. As she watched him head up the path toward the rest of the Quarters, she noticed the heaviness in his carriage that was all too familiar, for he had been heavy with a silent grief for years after the death of his older brother. Just when Gabriel seemed to be relaxing into his manhood, having completed his studies and becoming more focused on his love for Ella, the letter had arrived, stating exactly what they all knew in their hearts it would say. And yet, the letter also brought along a new heaviness for Gabriel to bear. With all of her might, all of her will and drive, Martha was determined that he would not bear his burden alone. She knew that soon she would have to make a move that would change not only his life but hers as well and the mere thought of the outcome stole her breath.

To know and understand Gabriel Loveman, one would have to know and understand as much as possible about the entire Loveman clan, a small family consisting of a father, a mother, and their two sons, along with an uncle, who had no wife and no children of his own. Gabriel's father, John Loveman, though a man of few words, was the force of strength for his close-knit family. A deep-brown skinned man and handsome by all accounts, he wasn't the largest man and stood only five feet, eleven inches tall, but what John Loveman lacked in height, he made up for in genuineness and integrity. Anyone who knew him would describe him as a pleasant and considerate man, a man known to work hard, without complaining. Though he had never drawn any negative attention from the tyrant he worked for, nor from any of his peers, his demeanor suggested courage and dignity and he was counted as one of the most upright men amongst those he lived and dwelled. He was also known for his beautiful tenor and his tendency to break out in song whenever and wherever his spirit was moved. A voice that was both delicate and robust, John Loveman's singing was often the most magnificent occurrence in the typically oppressive days spent on the Peterson Plantation and his family and friends often found themselves grateful for his willingness to sing or hum throughout the laborious day.

More than anything, though, John Loveman was held in high regard for his devoted love for his family and for his obvious adoration of his wife, Rosalee Loveman. For years, they were the most admired, the most envied couple in the Quarters. Until life dealt them a shattering blow, many of the friends and neighbors had looked to them as the mark of the best life had to offer to descendants of slaves who remained in the South, laboring in fields they did not own, producing crops for profits that would support and enhance the lives of people who hated them. There was no denying the weariness and the drudgery of the life of a Southern sharecropper, whose life and days were spent in a manner very akin to the lives and days of their parents and grandparents, who themselves had been slaves to parents and grandparents of the man who now owned the land and the cabin John and Rosalee called home. Both being descendants of the first slaves purchased by the Peterson dynasty, John and Rosalee grew up alongside one another in the field. One would be inclined to say they were childhood friends except they grew up on a place, in a time, when colored people were negated a childhood. Instead of engaging in the kind of play and frolic that usually establishes playmates and friendships, John and Rosalee had formed their relationship in the cotton patch, laboring under a relentless sun and though neither could recall exactly the day when they met, they both readily admitted that they had grown up together.

When Robert Peterson decided John was of the age that he should take a wife and move into his own cabin, his parents called on Rosalee's parents and a match was made. Unlike most marriages that were formed in the Quarters, however, John and Rosalee's was just as much out of love as it was convenience. They had jumped the broom a few days later, after the day's work had ended and from the time they crossed the threshold of their little cabin, the two of them had been inseparable. Rosalee doted on John, she always had, for as long as anyone could remember and John endeavored to do whatever he could to make her happy and to give her the best life possible. Even after the roughest, the most strenuous of days in the field, they could find laughter among themselves.

Like most plantation owners, Robert Peterson had an arrangement with the colored people who worked on his property, from sunrise to sunset, without any actual, tangible pay for their labor. In return for their work, he allowed his laborers to live in what he referred to as cabins. Actually, the homes he provided to his workforce were the same tiny, two-to-three room shacks that had housed slaves his father and grandfather owned. Nevertheless, Robert Peterson, in exchange for their labor, allowed them to live in the Quarters, in their tiny homes, charging their rent against the pay they earned in the field. He also provided them with food, furniture, and clothing, all of which was meager and minimal. Still, somehow, year after year, each family that worked for him failed to earn enough money to cover the cost of the provisions, which meant they were bound to the Peterson Plantation for the next year and would be so bound unless and until they produced enough crops to earn enough profit to pay the debt owed to Robert Peterson for the allowances he provided to them. And although he never so much as paid them a dime for their labor, their indebtedness meant that, legally, they were not slaves. They were sharecroppers, laborers who slept in, ate and wore their share of the crops they produced.

Robert Peterson inherited the Peterson Plantation by default from his father, the late Richard Peterson, Sr., who, by all accounts, was one of the most shrewd businessmen of the pre-Civil War South. His plantation encompassed a great portion of the most fertile land in a State that his forefathers had settled. Thousands of acres of the greenest fields and most ample orchards set upon slight hills that rolled on and on and into one another for stretches of miles and the Peterson Plantation was a pillar of the financial market that extended far beyond the surrounding counties and even across the state's lines. Renown as one of the largest and most productive farmers in the south, year after year, Richard Peterson, through his land and his laborers yielded the most ample supply of hearty fruits and vegetables and his cotton fields were the source of material from the most notable clothing and manufacturing companies. Rumor had it that he even traded with a few companies abroad, including France and Italy.

Richard Peterson considered himself a good man, a lover of mankind, because, amongst his counterparts and throughout his home state and those surrounding, he had the most accommodating and most heavily populated of slave quarters. When the Civil War ended with the South's defeat and the liberation of the slaves, he unlike his neighbors, did not suffer the economic ruin from the end of slavery. He was among an elite group of pragmatists who had accepted the inevitable fall of the South long before his fellow statesmen and countrymen. Before his slaves heard any declaration of freedom and, thus, began to imagine life beyond his plantation, Richard Peterson met with each of slave family and offered freedom and land. He sat them all down, together and told them of his new idea of family and prosperity and how his wealth would extend to them and to their families. A few years before the war's end, in anticipation of the likely outcome, Richard Peterson set each slave on his property free and gave each family their own plot of land. He even put the transactions in writing. In each meeting, he explained how what he was doing was a divine but also very dangerous act on his part and then he had each newly freed slave pledge their loyalty to him, swearing them to secrecy. The man commonly referred to as "Old Man Peterson" explained in grave detail how if word got out that he had given niggers land, his very life could be taken and all that he owned and was now seeking to share would assuredly be destroyed. So in secrecy, he freed his slaves and conveyed his lands. With each transaction, he explained to the new landowners the cost of maintaining the land and the cost of production. Each man received the same explanation as to how the land belonged to them, although they would not be able to openly hold title, for any such public knowledge could get them all killed.

Time and time again, the older residents of the Quarters would recant the story of their liberation, to their offspring, usually in what manifested as plea to those tempted to flee from plantation life to remain and await the expected time of reckoning. In the darkest of days, with flare and exaggeration, the children of the former slaves were told how they were future landowners, that they labored for their own sake-that no matter how horrible life seemed to be from day to day, they were to be ever mindful that they were actually a free people. With immense forethought and self-serving strategy, Richard Peterson had convinced the same people he had enslaved that, without having to be required by the law to do so, he would provide all of the necessities for their farming operation- that because they had no money, they could all pay him back with labor, of course, and when their debt to him was paid in full, subsequent profits would then be saved on their behalf until a day came when the secret covering their agreement could be removed. This illusion of freedom and land ownership was enough for the older ones and for most younger ones, even those who sometimes questioned their circumstances.

Now here it was, over forty years since the end of the war, and that day had yet to come. The land did not belong to them, not a single square foot, and the only way to realize their ownership was to pay off the debt to Richard Peterson, and after he died, his son, Robert. The constant threat to their own lives that was once rooted in ownership of their bodies was now rooted in their debt to the Peterson family. That they would ever actually own a portion of the Peterson estate was a lie, of course, perhaps the cruelest of lies. Because Old Man Peterson set them free, they were bound. Because he gave them land, they owed him the cost of living on the same ground they worked.

There's an old saying that when you know better, you do better and the families that worked the fields of the Peterson plantation did not know any better when they labored year after year only to find themselves even more indebted to the Peterson clan. They did not know any better when they scolded, sometimes even beat their off-spring for questioning their way of life, or even worse, denouncing their loyalty to what looked like, felt like and each and every day seemed like slavery.

With a plight as miserable as the one of a Southern sharecrop-pers, one might be inclined to confuse the arrangement with slavery, which is the very reason why Robert Peterson took advantage of any opportunity to remind his employees that they were, indeed, a free people and, thus, free to reject the arrangement he had in place for them and free to leave the Peterson Plantation in order to seek a better life, somewhere else. The only cost for doing so would be their well-being and, more than likely, they would pay the cost with their very own lives.

A hopeful man, John Loveman lived for the day when he would work himself out of the debt he owed to the owner of the plantation where his family had always lived. His father's dying declaration to him had been that he was the right and truthful owner of the plot of land that housed the cabin the Loveman's had occupied since days of slavery. His grandfather had been one of those gathered the day the abolishment of slavery had been announced, the day the great lie was first told, the lie that if the newly freed people stayed on and worked the land, they would be doing so for the benefit of their loved ones and that the Peterson Plantation would no longer profit from unpaid labor. He hadn't just uttered words to demonstrate his sincerity and to convince his former slaves to remain on their homeland. To entice them, to compel the people to continue their labor in his cotton and tobacco fields, he told them they would become landowners, themselves, and had even gone so far as to draw up deeds that conveyed the land from him to them. Each man with a family and a cabin was given an unsigned, undated deed, with the promise that once he paid the balance owed to the Peterson family for providing them the clothes and food they would need to get through the planting and harvesting seasons, the deeds would be legally executed. Now, two generations later, John Loveman understood that the Peterson family would never honor that declaration made so long ago. He had to wonder if the old man who stood on the porch that day practically begging "his niggers" to stay and conduct business with him for all of their sake ever really meant to keep that promise to "do right" by those who elected to stay on and work for him.

Still, as doubtful as he was that such a day would ever come, John Loveman had held onto the deed that he had been given at his father's deathbed. The poor man had received the tattered document in similar fashion from his beloved father, a former slave who had lived and worked with an immense hope that the words on the paper would actually be honored and he would, indeed, be a landowner and a man in control of his own destiny.

The hope faded with each transfer from generation to generation and John Loveman did not behold his grandfather's expectations. He worked to provide food and shelter to the family he loved and he committed himself to appreciating life as it stood. He was a practical man, a man who meant what he said and only said what he meant. He told anyone he knew that he lived only to care for his family, to love and cherish his wife and to provide and protect his precious boys. For years, he kept his word to do so, until the day came when his paternal protection fell short and life took away the gift of song from his voice.

Years before, when John Loveman made his vow to love, honor and keep Rosalee he not only meant every word, he took his oath to her and God to heart. As far as he was concerned having Rosalee in his life was the best thing that could happen to a man in his circumstances and he loved her beyond measure. Rosalee Loveman was a woman with a heart of gold, filled with both laughter and goodness. All of her life, Rosalee Loveman had been so many things to so many people. As a child, she was her parent's delight and though they died when she was very young, she grew up knowing she had been loved very much by both of them and she carried their love and her memory of them in her heart. Rosalee was proof of just how much of an impact loving parents can have on a person's life, no matter the social situation, no matter their financial status. As a young lady, she was a sure friend and her peers appreciated her. She was wise beyond her years and her elders entrusted her with the information that was passed from generation to generation, the kind of information that made for the best welfare for the people of the Quarters. She shadowed midwives and pastors, who taught her what to do in times of need and crisis and she could often be found watching her elders as they cooked or sewed or took care of the sick. And she was a quick study. She was strong yet caring. She was cautious, but engaging and she was gracious, delightful person in all of her comings and goings. After she married John Loveman, she instantly became the kind of wife the best of men hoped for and an ideal mate for her beloved husband.

Rosalee had grown up beside John Loveman and their love was as natural as the wind, as easy as breathing for both of them. Their marriage and the birth of their two sons were the balancing factors of both of their lives, the joy from which overwhelmed the challenges of living on and working the lands on the Peterson Plantation, under the cruel control of Robert Peterson.

Until the tragedy of her life occurred, Rosalee had always been a happy woman who could always be counted on to lift the spirits of everyone around her. Her round babyish face seemed to constantly possess the most infectious smile and she had the unmatched ability to lighten even the gloomiest of occasions. She was large in stature, with an attractive and curvaceous frame. She towered over most other women and was almost as tall as her husband. Despite her size, Rosalee Loveman was anything but intimidating and her presence was inviting and reassuring. Her eyes were once huge, vibrant shiny windows to what was once the most liveliest of souls. Her lively spirit and heart of gold were contagious to everyone in the Quarters and neighbors and friends looked to her as a guiding light in what was hardly ever anything but a dim and dread-filled existence. All the more, her positive attitude was rooted, not in naivety, but in wisdom, for she was insightful and knowledgeable about the ways of the world they lived in and her neighbors and friends marveled at her willingness to choose happiness despite the misery surrounding her life on the Peterson Plantation. They were amazed by what seemed to be her daily decision to live life to the fullest and to spread cheer and joy to those she knew and loved. Days on end in the sweltering heat of the crop fields, Rosalee Loveman would teach, preach, and encourage her family and neighbors through their seemingly never-ending workdays.

Rosalee Loveman had long been described as the sweetest woman in the Quarters and hardly ever was she the subject of jealousy or envy, despite the fact that most women longed for a husband as kind and faithful as John and for children as gifted and good-looking as her two boys. Never one to boast, when complimented about her family, Rosalee would quickly turn the admiration right around, so that any friend or neighbor always left feeling better about their own families. She delighted in her husband's love and when the situation called for her to take on the care and nurturing of her brother-in-law, she did so without even the slightest complaint. In her mind, she existed to make her husband's life better, sweeter, and if taking in his brother gave her darling man peace of mind, Rosalee endeavored to make their home his home. Though the arrangement was considered odd by most, the respect the people of the Quarters had for Rosalee overrode any inclination toward gossip and suspicion. Folks simply figured that John and Rosalee had a good reason for allowing another grown man to live with them, to burden them with the extra costs of food and clothing. Most women would have objected and even if futile, the objection would have carried forward in the manner in which she treated and engaged with such a cumbersome addition to the family. Rosalee Loveman was not like most women, though. She was joyful, kind and gracious in her words and in her actions. Some people are just natural-born givers and Rosalee Loveman spent her days and nights giving to everyone she knew and loved, especially the menfolk of her immediate family.

When she gave birth to her oldest child, Rosalee had fully expected her son Benjamin to be the first of many children. Yet when she miscarried not once, not twice but seven treacherous times afterwards, she refused to be bitter or sad. Benjamin was a blessing and both she and her husband were thankful that the good Lord had blessed them with such a lovely child. They had witnessed the horror of John's brother's unimaginable loss of not only a child, who was born stillborn, but also the loss of his young wife who died only hours after giving birth. They refused to tempt God by dwelling too much on their own miscarried pregnancies. Rosalee was beyond content with her son. Overall, she was happy and despite their humble, really miserable, living and working conditions, she was a woman who appreciated what she had. When she became pregnant, again, six years after Benjamin was born, she did not allow herself to become overly hopeful. As a matter of fact, she hardly mentioned the child she was carrying, nor did anyone else, for fear she should experience, yet again, another miscarriage. However, Rosalee did pray, for she was a faithful woman, who always maintained an earnest hope and trust in God. Throughout her entire pregnancy with her youngest son, Rosalee prayed that God would bless her and give her strength and that He would especially bless the child she was carrying. When Gabriel Loveman was born, Rosalee knew right away that her prayers had been answered.

For thirteen years after Gabriel's birth, Rosalee considered herself the most fortunate woman on the Peterson Plantation and she didn't compare herself to just the women who lived in the Quarters. She knew herself to be the most blessed woman in all her surroundings, white or black, and she was. She had the most loving husband the entire farm over and the two most wonderful sons a mother could ever raise. Those years were the happiest of her life. The years following were to be the saddest.

David Loveman, the younger brother of John Loveman, had spent most of his adult life living with his elder brother and his family. Although at first notice any observer would relate the two brothers, for they very much looked alike, but where John was quiet and reserved, David was robust and hearty in character. Regardless of his mood or any activity at hand, John's eyes seemed to hold a consistent glare, while David's eyes always seem to dance as he talked, and especially when he laughed. David was known throughout the Quarters for his lighthearted manner and his ability to see the good in just about anyone or any situation. He was a welcomed addition to the Loveman family unit and, more than an uncle, he was a father figure and a friend to his beloved nephews, who he loved as if they were his own children.

Although the notion was hardly ever spoken aloud, most folks on the Peterson Plantation attributed David's humor and jovial manner to him being just a little close to crazy. When he was just a young man, he had married a girl from a neighboring farm, a pretty girl, who, without question, loved and doted on him. When she and the baby the young couple was expecting died suddenly without warning only hours after a grueling, tormentous labor and delivery, David had become mad with grief. When his cabin burned to the ground the day afterwards, charring both of the deceased beyond any appropriateness for burial, just about everyone suspected that David had deliberately set the blaze and that he did so to avoid a burial ceremony. Many suspected his mind simply could not bear the thought of placing the woman he loved and their stillborn child in the same ground he would have to pass by day after day. While no one in the Quarters accused him outright, David was almost thrown off the property by Robert Peterson, who was livid at the destruction of property on his estate. John Loveman had pleaded on his brother's behalf, had explained to the infuriated plantation owner just how crazed David was with grief and pledged to be personally responsible for his brother from that day forward. In an act of graciousness, Robert Peterson tacked the value of the cabin onto John Loveman's debt balance and explained that, from that day forward, the payoff would thus be John's sole responsibility.

Though the decision that David would live with John and his family was made under dire circumstances, John was relieved to have his brother with him. He worried that if left alone, due to the extreme sadness over the death of his wife and child, David might harm himself. John and his wife had accepted David into their home with no resentment whatsoever. They patiently, gracefully nursed him back to wellness and after awhile, David became healthy enough to labor in the fields and contribute to the upkeep of their family. Although he would sometimes drift off into his own thoughts, for the most part, over the years, David regained his sense of humor and outgoing nature. He spent days working as hard as he could to assist his brother and sister-in-law with the family's needs and he lavished all of the love he had looked forward to showering on his own family onto John and Rosalee and even more so on their sons. Benjamin and Gabriel became the lights of his life and he made no qualms about his attachment to his beloved nephews.

David had spent years living with the grief that surrounded his thoughts of the woman he loved long ago and the child he never had a chance to know and care for. Just when the grief had seemed to reduce itself to nothing more than a hint of hurt, every now and again, David was introduced to a new grief, one that he wasn't sure his mind would allow him to overcome. The only possibility of sanity rested with his love and attention toward Gabriel, for after Benjamin's death the youngest member of the Loveman clan became the primary focus of David's love and hope. Nothing would ever fill the hole in his heart left from the loss of Benjamin, for as his name suggested, the darling lad had been the quintessential son of the south. As it turned out, southern society and tradition had governed both the birth and death of his nephew and all that remained of him was the loving memory of his life held captive in the hearts and minds of the family who mourned him without mention, but deeply, emphatically, all day, every day of their lives. As much as David missed Benjamin, he worried over Gabriel, worried that his only nephew would lose his life, too, if not physically, mentally and spiritually, if his own hope for the boy was not realized.

Without question, Benjamin Loveman, the first son born to John and Rosalee, was the most beautiful person to grace the fields and foothills of the Peterson Plantation. By declaration of all those who lived in Chester County and surrounding areas, from the time he entered the world up until his premature departure from life, Benjamin had been the best looking man they had ever seen. As if his good looks weren't enough to draw constant attention, he also had a radiant, infectious personality that made him the most popular person in the Quarters.

By the time he reached adulthood, he stood a wondrous six feet six inches tall and with broad chest and lean legs, he looked nothing less than a caramel-brown Adonis. His eyes were hazel and huge and his gigantic smile gave way to an almost perfect set of teeth. Benjamin Loveman was a happy, talented young man, who was full of life and who constantly exhibited good humor, wit and charm. He had a lifelong passion for farming, for growing things, and an overall appreciation for life. Benjamin Loveman was not prone to complaint or self-pity and usually only spoke about the beauty that each human being and each living creature beheld. More than anyone else, Benjamin talked about the genius of his baby brother and how he considered himself the luckiest person alive to be Gabriel's big brother.

To Benjamin, Gabriel represented the future and he believed himself to be the one designated by God to nurture, cultivate, and protect that future. Though he was seven years older than Gabriel, Benjamin bestowed upon his younger, marvelous sibling a great respect and, in many ways, recognized him as his equal. While he taught him about the land, plantation life, the ways of the white man and the plight of the colored man, he did so in a way that was informative and instructional, but never condescending. Though he himself never cared for reading and writing, Benjamin recognized Gabriel's academic abilities, and understood his little brother's natural brilliance.

A genius of sorts, himself, his own God-given gifts were revealed through both his farming skills and his vocal talents. Like his father, Benjamin also had the glorious gift of song and sang just as much as he talked. All who were fortunate enough to ever have heard him sing agreed that his voice contained an exhilarating and nearly perfect pitch. With seemingly minimal effort, Benjamin would hum and sing hymns with a volume that carried his song magically throughout the Quarters, deep into the fields, over and beyond the hills of the Peterson Plantation and up into the great beyond. Even when he finished the delivery of whichever of his favorite hymns he had chosen to place into the air, the remnants of the song seemed to linger on in the hollows of the countless trees and over into the bowels of the fields where the toiling and tiring seemed to never end. Once delivered, Benjamin's songs loomed in the air, long after he finished singing, graciously remaining there until he lifted his voice again with another hymn.

From the time Benjamin had been old enough to learn the words and the melody, he and his father had gifted the people of the Quarters with his father's favorite hymn at the close of many days in the field. No one tired of hearing them sing the song and even on the few occasions of leisure, when crowds were gathered at the base of the large oak or sitting around in conversation a porch of a cabin, if John and Benjamin both happened to be present, someone would always ask the father-son duo to sing "their song". Each rendition of the song would begin with John taking the lead. In his smooth, even tenor, he would sing each word of the hymn with precision and deliberation...

I was sinking deep in sin
Far from the peaceful shore
Very deeply stained within
Sinking to rise no more
But the Master of the sea
Heard my despairing cry
And from the waters lifted
Now safe am I...

And then Benjamin in his dynamic baritone would join him for the chorus and together they would croon.

LOVE LIFTED (EVEN ME)
LOVE LIFTED (EVEN ME)
WHEN NOTHING ELSE COULD HELP
LOVE LIFTED ME (EVEN ME)
LOVE LIFTED (EVEN ME)
LOVE LIFTED (EVEN ME)
WHEN NOTHING ELSE COULD HELP
LOVE LIFTED ME (EVEN ME)

The loveliest part, the part of the song their audience most enjoyed hearing was the second verse, not just because of the poignancy and the beauty of the lyrics, but also because John and Benjamin, father and son, blended their voices so harmoniously, so perfectly, singing the whole verse in unison, that the listener could barely tell one voice from the other. Singing in glorious pitch, the two of them sounded like one pristine vocal instrument and hearts and souls stirred when they raised their volume and sang the next verse, together, with certainty and conviction.

All my heart to Him I give
Ever to Him I'll cling
In His blessed presence live
Ever His praise to sing
Love so mighty and true
Merits my soul's best song
Faithful, loving service too
To Him belongs

By the time they finished the second verse, everyone gathered around, those who could carry a tune, and those who could not, would join in for the final chorus and all the Quarters it seemed would gleefully sing.

LOVE LIFTED ME (EVEN ME)
LOVE LIFTED ME (EVEN ME)
WHEN NOTHING ELSE COULD HELP
LOVE LIFTED ME (EVEN ME)
LOVE LIFTED ME (EVEN ME)
LOVE LIFTED ME (EVEN ME)
WHEN NOTHING ELSE COULD HELP
LOVE LIFTED ME (EVEN ME)

Often, the Loveman's performance was the best thing that happened to folks in the course of their days on the Peterson Plantation. And as Benjamin grew from boy to man, his voice matured in a way that perfected his duet with his beloved father. The last time folks heard them sing together, the song was so wonderfully delivered grown men had become visibly emotional and several women had wept out loud.

With Benjamin gone, the Quarters had lost the uplift the song brought and the joy of hearing the Lovemans singing so beautifully. Of course, Benjamin could not sing from the grave and his father had not sung since he had buried his child. His heartbreak had silenced his voice and he could not imagine singing solo and without the delightful company of his darling boy. Sadly, the death of Benjamin Loveman had taken all of the music out of the air of the Peterson Plantation and the void created by his death was felt throughout the whole of the Quarters. However, no one felt the void as much as Gabriel. No one needed him as much and missed him as much as his little brother, who, with the receipt of the acceptance letter, felt his absence more than ever.

Chapter Six

BALLOONS AND BARRIERS

The breaking dusk was the kind of sky that only happens every now and again, especially during that particular time of year. The summer's heat lent itself to the blending of oranges and browns right at the edge of day and the sun shrank into the thinnest line of shimmer in the middle of the golden bronze sky. Sometimes, the sight was marvelous and breathtaking. That evening, however, lingering sunset loomed in a most unspectacular way. Like everything else on the Peterson Plantation, the summer's eve skyline was just another backdrop for Gabriel's burdens. As he sat under what was once his favorite tree, in what was once his favorite resting place, Gabriel no more appreciated the beauty of the sky before him than he did the coolness of the shade offered by the massive oak he sat beneath. He had no more favorites. The letter had taken all of them away.

Gone was his favorite path, the one that led from the back of the fields down to the schoolhouse, the one that was lined with groves of trees full of peaches and apples and pears, all ripe for the picking. Gone was his favorite porch, the one that folks gathered on at the close of the work day to laugh and swap tall tales and to take refuge in one another's company before settling in for the evening. Gone was his favorite creek, the one that he and Ella sat alongside holding hands almost every Saturday afternoon when their work was done. The creekwater gave Gabriel a sense of security and served as a calming, reassuring soundstage for the rare occasion when he spoke his mind aloud. He would wade in until the water met his kneecaps and turn himself to the bank, while Ella sat perched atop a huge boulder, listening intensely and patiently, as he told her of his dream to get away from the South, away from all of the horror of the life he was expected to endure and to go off to school and earn a degree. He spoke of his plans for a profession that would pay him the money he so desperately needed to get his family and her away from the Peterson Plantation forever.

Ella never said much. She hardly ever commented at all, as Gabriel ranted on and on about what he could do, if he could just get away. And though he may as well have been declaring his desire to be President of the United States of America, so far-fetched was any such dream for a young man of color, Ella, never, ever uttered a word of doubt of discouragement. Because she never considered his dreams to be far-fetched or unattainable, her silence in that regard was organic and supportive. Week after week, she sat up on that great big rock and just listened and when he tired of talking and telling about his plans for a better life for them all, she would listen to him talk about his big brother and about how much and why he missed him-about how nobody, except her, maybe, understood him, believed in him like Benjamin did and also how his absence meant that Gabriel had to be the brawn and the brain of the Loveman Family. Ella listened each Saturday, as the love of her life went from planning to grieving back to planning, while wading in his favorite creek. That time with Ella was by far Gabriel's most precious moments. Yet, now that the letter had come, even those memories, even thoughts of Ella and her constant show of love and support failed to bring Gabriel any peace of mind or comfort.

As he sat there with his head pressed ever so firmly into the base of his beautiful oak, Gabriel could see all of his favorite things about the farm. He could see the Goodman's porch, empty that night, barren of company and laughter. He could see the path that led to the school yard, now cluttered with rotting, stinking fruit and he could see the creek, which looked more like a thin mud and a haven for mosquitoes, crickets and frogs than a cool, refreshing retreat that helped wash away his blues. The letter that lined the inside of his shirt weighed heavily on Gabriel's heart and mind that evening, serving as a stark highlighter of what his life on the Peterson Plantation actually was and would be, all the days of his life, if he never left. Because of the letter, all the things that made life bearable, all those favorite places and favorite times seemed so very plain and ordinary, even bleak, for they were minimal and miniscule in relation to the harsh realities of his daily existence on a cotton farm, where slavery was no longer legally in effect but where freedom, actual freedom, was still a mere fantasy for people of color. The letter emphasized those realities, made them stand out in Gabriel's mind and brought forth the piercing truth that life as he knew it was miserable and always would be. What pained Gabriel all the more was facing the cruel truth that even his love for Ella, which was certain and without compromise, even that one beautiful reality would fail to balance the weight of hopelessness that was sure to dwell within him if he did not leave the South. The thought of staying pained him almost as much as Benjamin's death.

Gabriel had never recovered from his brother's murder. If he chose to forego acting on the contents of the letter, grieving the loss of his only sibling along with the loss of his future would be his plight. If he went where the letter's content would take him, mourning Benjamin and enduring the distance leaving would place between him and Ella and his family would be his plight. Yet, the latter option offered him opportunity in return and Gabriel found himself wondering if opportunity served as the cure for grief, all the while knowing deep within that there was no such actual cure for that kind of broken heart. At most, the opportunity could serve as a viable treatment for his despair.

Sitting there under his tree, Gabriel pulled out the letter and read it once again. For the past few weeks, doing so whenever he could had brought him hope and a little happiness. That evening, though, reading his college acceptance letter only brought sadness and a sense of emptiness upon him. Maybe, his melancholy was due to the fact that there were only three weeks or so left before the academic year started, three weeks left for him to make a final decision. Maybe, he was feeling the trauma of Ella's announcement to him that she could not imagine going with him and leaving her mother behind. Or maybe, it was just one of those days where life on the Peterson Plantation was so apparent that Gabriel could not help but feel drained and depressed. Maybe, it was because he was tired beyond his usual tiredness at that time of day. But as he sat there, reading the acceptance letter, once again, with the last hint of the day's light fading into the dusk of the eve, Gabriel felt like the weight of the whole world was on his chest. The more and more he read the letter, the more consumed he became with an overwhelming sense of defeatedness and guilt.

How could he even think about leaving? How in the world would his beloved father and dear mother manage without him? There were no answers that came to his mind that remotely suggested they would survive day to day plantation work without him, even if they first were spared the wrath Robert Peterson threatened would fall upon them if Gabriel left them behind. All Gabriel could think about was his own tiredness, how even with his youthfulness and strength, he felt exhausted and physically broken after every day's labor in the field. His mother and father worked just as much in the same fields, everyday, his uncle, too. Their bodies were beaten and broken by decades of intensive work, with little relief and hardly anytime off. Their hearts carried the weariness of grief and resignation and so they moved about steadily, but slowly. Gabriel did as much work as all three of them put together and his labor kept them from plummeting further into debt with Robert Peterson.

Beyond the matter of working the fields, how could Gabriel so much as consider leaving them knowing the void in their life that yet remained due to their loss of Benjamin? How could he cause them to suffer the heartbreak of losing him, not to death but to distance? Leaving would more than likely mean never returning and possibly never seeing them again. The very thought was agonizing and the ache in Gabriel's heart settled, stubbornly. Then he thought about what his leaving would mean to Ella and the ache seemed to spread throughout his chest and spill over into his guts, which were made nauseous at the thought of a life without her. Besides his brilliance, she was his one true thing. As much as he wanted to further his education, as much as he wanted to explore and live a life away from the drudgery of the South, Gabriel knew he would never love another woman the way he loved Ella.

They were kindred spirits. Not just because they understood one another's sadness. More than that, Gabriel trusted Ella and the only person he trusted more was dead and gone. Besides, their bond held a different kind of trust. He trusted her, not because she looked after him as Benjamin once did, but because, somehow, Gabriel knew she loved him beyond his brilliance. He could tell her of his fears and still know she saw him as courageous. He could express his resentfulness of his family's circumstances to her and still know she saw him as loyal. He could be quiet with Ella and not utter a word and she understood, still, exactly what his quietness meant. She understood his silence. Going through life with her was the one notion that made the idea of sharecropping and farm life bearable. Going through life without her was the one possibility that he knew he would always regret and mourn, even if he realized his plan and went away to school without her. He knew that if he left, he would probably never come back and since she had devoted her life to caring for her mother, there was a chance he would never see her again. They both knew that Gabriel's hope was also their shared heartbreak. If

Gabriel hadn't realized the enormity of their plight before, Ella had made their dilemma clear the afternoon of the Fourth of July picnic.

For several days, neither of them had mentioned the letter or the possibility of his departure. Ella had made an effort to keep any anguish she was feeling hidden, as she in no way wanted to discourage Gabriel or cause him to feel any more guilt than he was already suffering. Doing so, however, was far from an easy feat. For Ella, doing so was a continual exercise of putting the one she loved over herself. If she thought of herself at all, it seemed, she would run the risk of failing her love for Gabriel, because thinking of her feelings and what her life without him would become would only tempt her to beg him to stay. Somehow, she knew that she didn't even have to beg, though she might if, for any length of time, she thought about how much she needed him and what a huge part of her life Gabriel consumed. Ella knew that if she simply asked Gabriel not to go, if she merely suggested that his doing so would be the wrong or hurtful decision, he would not leave. That's how much he loved her. That was an undeniable fact that Ella knew and cherished.

From the first day she met Gabriel Loveman, Ella knew she was protected, cared about and loved. She never doubted his devotion, never had a reason to wonder if his feelings for her were sincere and long-lasting. Even when he shut out most of the world after he lost his beloved brother, Gabriel had kept her close. He allowed her to dwell in that place where no one else could reach him, that place where he seemed to cave deep, deep inside himself, into the tiniest cracks of his mind and into the narrowest crevices of his heart. When Gabriel went inside himself no one could reach him, not his faithful teacher and mentor, who he greatly appreciated, not his father, who he held in the highest esteem, not the uncle who often held his confidence and not even his dear, sweet mother, who he greatly adored. Gabriel's retreat inward meant everyone was denied access to his beauty and brilliance and though he was never cruel or disrespectful, his ability to close off emotionally and shut down on his loved ones was resound and effective. Even though they desperately wanted to be connected to him at all times, they understood why Gabriel, oftentimes, would retreat into himself and place an invisible "keep out" sign around his psyche. Even if they didn't always understand why or even if they weren't always prepared, whenever he embarked upon what sometimes would be days of silence, Gabriel's family always respected their darling boy's unusual yet obvious need to close himself off to the world and people around him. Ella, however, was exempted from his disconnection. Whenever Gabriel closed himself off, he did so in a way that placed Ella on the inside of the emotional barrier that kept everyone else out. She resided there alongside him during his stints into his dark places, not because he allowed her to or even because he wanted her to be there, but because her existence alongside him, physically and mentally, was of the most natural design. Gabriel could neither allow nor disallow her presence, even in the most intricate and delicate havens of his inner-being. She was his soulmate, if ever there was such a thing and their unity was apparent and accepted by everyone who knew them.

From the day they first met, Gabriel and Ella were inseparable. Where he went, she went. When he played, she played and when he studied, she studied. As they grew older, they grew closer and courtship was far too shallow an endeavor to describe their interaction with one another. Their love evolved and matured as nature and their personalities commanded. Physically, they were a handsome couple and love seemed to illuminate around them whenever they were together or near one another- love and sadness, as well. The older folks in the Quarters did not frown upon their interaction, even when they were just a boy and girl. From the start, everybody- Gabriel's family, Ella's mother and aunt, the elders, even their childhood friends and schoolmates- acknowledged the preciousness of their affection for one another. Everyone trusted that whatever developed between the two of them, whenever and wherever, such would happen as fate dictated. Most everyone around them knew and accepted any effort at compromising their involvement, any attempt to stagnate or retard their ever-growing adoration would not only fail, but, quite obviously, also would bring injury to two souls that had already been gravely injured. No one who knew them wanted to run the risk of further harm to two people who had suffered so very much so very early in life. The least the world could do was let them have each other. And so as a little boy and little girl, as preteens, when boys and girls usually, intentionally remained separate from one another and as young adults, Gabriel and Ella had remained inseparable. Nothing seemed to come between them, nothing, that is, except Gabriel's genius and his dream to go away from the life they lived in Chester County, on Peterson Plantation.

In her heart, Ella knew she would not hold him back. She could never do that to him. She knew what he had given to her all the years since she first met him needed to be shared with so many others who had yet to discover the beauty of Gabriel's intelligence. Ella knew that his genius and his graciousness would make the world a better place, as soon as he entered into that realm of the world where possibility could transform into reality. She fully understood that the Peterson Plantation was not a part of that world and that his gifts could only be put to use beyond the gate that separated their dreadful life on the farm from that awaiting world. She was sure that Gabriel had to walk through that gate and away from her, as sure as she was that she loved him more than anything or anyone else, except the good Lord above. She would go with him, if she could, but to dream that unlikely dream was a waste of time and only made the thought of him leaving feel even more unbearable. Instead, Ella thought about all the great things her love would do, all the people he would help and all the pride and joy everyone who knew him would feel as a result of his greatness. In her mind, if she couldn't have him for the rest of her life, at least she would have the joy of knowing that she loved him enough not to hold him back and that, perhaps, in some small way, by encouraging him to go, she, too, would be a part of something good, better yet, something extraordinarily great.

∞

Gabriel's potential and his new opportunity was exactly what Ella had been thinking about, as they sat on their tattered blanket that Fourth of July, when all of a sudden, everyone around them began to bustle about and point toward the sky. Before she could ask Gabriel if he knew what all the fuss was about, she saw the object of alarm. During a civic lesson from Ms. Martha, a few years earlier, they had learned about the invention of the hot air balloon, but never before had anyone living on the Peterson Plantation seen such a sight as a gigantic red rubber bubble, larger than life, it seemed, floating across the sky, in celebration of the nation's birthday. The sight of the flying balloon was breathtaking and without hesitation, Ella grabbed her chest, bent herself forward over her knees and began a rocking motion. She was so captivated, she didn't realize that she was speaking her thoughts aloud, but when Gabriel heard her say, whisper, rather, that she wished she could just jump into the balloon and drift off far away from Robert Peterson's land, something inside him shook and his belly tightened in a knot that cramped him to his core.

"I got my balloon, Ella. Got it right here," he said, touching his chest where the letter was kept on the inside of his shirt. "I just don't know if I should get in and fly off, go away from this place where I'm surely needed. Or go away from you."

Even now, as he sat alone, at the close of the day, under the tree that sheltered him from the sun but not from his desperate thoughts, Gabriel could hear Ella's response as if she was sitting there beside him, speaking as anxiously and as passionately as she did that day, when the balloon floated high above them and off into the distance as she responded to his revelation.

In a rushed tone, barely above a whisper, she asked, "How in the world could you have a balloon, something that would take you away and set you free from the hell we live- how, Gabriel, can you have a way out of here and not use it?"

She tilted her head and implored, further. "You mean to tell me, ME...." she stopped, searching her heart for exactly the right words and, then, slowly, more deliberately, she began to speak again.

"I know you. I know what you want. I know you want it more than you want me. And crazy as I am for feeling the way I do, but I want it for you, too." Straightening her back and adjusting her dress in preparation for what she needed to say next, Ella drew a deep breath and looked straight into Gabriel's eyes. She needed to know he was listening and taking in what she was about to say. She would only be able to say it once.

"I love you, want you, more than dignity will allow me to say, more than you will probably ever know. But as much as I want you, I want that for you even more. My one chance for a happy moment in this here miserable life is to be able to see you climb inside that balloon of yours and fly away off to the wonderful places it will take you, places where you belong, where you can be all that you was born to be, Gabriel."

Turning her face away from him and looking downward, Ella began to rock back and forth again, as if she was egging herself on, keeping her momentum, since what was on her mind was so very difficult to say, yet so very necessary for him to hear. She raised her voice a bit, making sure he could hear every word.

"Ain't no way you can be you, the whole you, the real you, on Peterson Plantation. This place is too small, too wicked, too much the same plain old wretched way of life, day after day. And everybody I know, every single person I know, for whatever Godly or evil reason, belongs here. Everybody except you. I know there are plenty of things telling you that you belong here, too. I know one of those things is your love for me. But even that is a lie, a sweet lie, but a lie, still, Gabriel, when that love tells you to stay here, especially if you now really have a way to leave. You sit here calling it your balloon. Okay. Whatever. We both know what it is and we both you you've always had it. We didn't even need the letter to tell us that. All that letter does is let you know you can use what God blessed you with to get away from here."

Ella became still again and gazed up into the sky, as if she was searching for the hot air balloon that was now nowhere in sight. When she next spoke, her voice was filled with pride and amazement.

"Gabriel, you have done what most white folks around here will never do. You've gone and got yourself accepted to college. Ain't that what they call it? And that school accepted you because those folks up there now know what all of us here on this farm have always known about you and that is you are special. You have the extra something else that most of us will never have in this life. As a matter of fact, we consider ourselves lucky to just share the same space with you. I feel special. I feel like my extra something else is that I am the one who loves you most of all. And everybody loves you."

Looking back Gabriel's way, Ella took in another breath and lowered her voice back down to the bare whisper. She was spent but she had to say everything on her mind.

"Your Ma, your Pa and your Uncle, Ms. Martha and all the neighbors, too. They all love you so much. But I believe I love you the most because I love you enough to be the one to look you in your face right now and say to you, Gabriel Loveman, that if you got a way out of here, if you can go and become everything the good Lord made you to be, if you got a balloon if that's what you want to call it, then shame on you if you don't climb inside of it and fly off away from everything and everybody here on the Peterson Plantation, including me."

Gabriel knew, as hard as telling him to leave must have been for Ella, she meant every word she uttered that afternoon, for the tears streaming down her cheeks and the way she collapsed into his arms when she was done confirmed what he already felt deep inside his

71

heart. Ella wanted whatever was best for him, even if she had to give him up in order for his best life to happen. As she shook and cried, Gabriel knew she wept for the loss she would surely suffer, if he listened to her. He also knew that all of her other losses, all of her past suffering made her strong and that ultimately she could bear the loss of their love and the union they would definitely have if he did not go. What Gabriel did not know, what remained quite uncertain was whether or not he could bear life without her.

In all the years that he had known her, loved her, Gabriel had never heard Ella say so much at one time. In his heart, he knew saying what she said took courage and that she spoke only out of sheer love and devotion. He knew more than anything else that she cared that much about him, cared enough to turn him loose and bid him farewell. Her sacrifice made him love her more, harder, and, as much as he had been yearning for her for quite some time, his passion for her was intensified beyond his imagination by her defiant declaration that she wanted him to make the choice that would leave her and their love behind.

Gabriel wanted to take Ella into his arms and explain to her all the thoughts that had been swirling around his mind since the moment he received the letter of acceptance. He wanted to tell her that more than their love compelled him to stay, that family loyalty and duty also weighed heavily against his ability to act on the letter. He wanted to tell her that money was more than a matter, rather not having money was another great wall between him and the places the letter could take him. More than that, more than any of those matters, Gabriel wanted to tell her about his fear. He knew that she was the one person he could trust to understand that he was afraid to go, not just because of what may happen to his family should he leave or what he would face if he left without coming up with the money he needed for housing and food. Gabriel knew Ella was the only person to whom he could confess that he was afraid to go and discover that perhaps he wasn't so special, after all- that he wasn't so

gifted and that he didn't actually possess that extraordinary something to give the world, although he had been told he did for as long
as he could remember. And though day in and day out Benjamin's
voice of encouragement still whispered constantly in the back of his
mind, Gabriel was afraid to go and risk letting Ella, Ms. Martha and
his family down. He knew that if he went off to school and failed
that he would become a disappointment to people who had already
been disappointed by life amply enough.

More than anything, though, Gabriel did not want to disappoint
his lost love, Benjamin. He couldn't imagine life without that whisper
of love and hope in his mind and, if he failed, he was sure he would
lose what was left of his connection with his big brother. If he stayed
on the farm, if he built and focused on the best life he could have
on the Peterson Plantation, he would always have that whisper of
hope. He would always have the certainty of being accepted into
college, which was an unthinkable accomplishment within itself. His
family would be safe and he would have the precious gift of Ella's
love and companionship for the rest of his days. That love, surely,
would comfort and, perhaps, quiet the pain he would carry, the pain
that is uniquely caused by the giving up of one's destiny. If he stayed,
he would always be brilliant and gifted. He could reduce his dreams
to just being the Loveman's son and to one day becoming Ella's
husband and hopefully the father of her children. He'd become just
another sharecropper, working unjustly and for the mere sake of a
meager existence. He'd be just another colored man in the South,
which would mean he would hardly exist at all. He would live life in
the shell so many other colored men lived in, since existing entirely
and fully was a danger to a man of color in the South, a very threat
to physical life and a frustration, emotionally and spiritually because a
human being cannot live a large life in the small space of oppression.
If he remained, Gabriel would undoubtedly have to dwindle down
to a man who accepted life for what it was rather what it should have
been and a man who moved through life quietly, drawing as little

attention to himself as possible. The reduction of the ambition of Gabriel Loveman would be a tragedy, indeed, but killing his dreams and accepting his station on the farm was a foreseeable plight and a life he could believed he could bear.

As he held Ella while she collected herself, Gabriel decided against trying to explain how he felt to her. He knew she was waiting for his answer and that she was probably in agony over her heartfelt release and instruction for him to get on with what she was sure to be the great life he was destined to live. As she nudged her nose into his chest and pressed herself into him as hard as she could, anticipating his response, she heard him say, quietly, slowly, with heavy breaths between his words, "Balloons don't always float, Baby. Sometimes, there just isn't enough air."

As Gabriel sat alone with his thoughts of going and staying, he could not escape the truth of Ella's words. She knew him better than anyone else, except he knew himself even better. Any thoughts of self-doubt or uncertainty were few and far between and they paled in comparison to Gabriel's true sense of self. If the dilemma was before any other man, one may have been inclined to think that he was not fully aware of his potential. But that was the difference in Gabriel. He knew. He seemed to know his whole life long. His knowledge of himself is what made his decision so intense, so grueling at heart. Should he go and make his mark on the world, one that was bound to make a difference in the countless lives of others or should he remain on the farm, caring for and working on behalf of those who loved and needed him, especially Ella. Though he had not spoken of the letter since the picnic, the decision before him plagued his mind all day, every day and he was consumed, overwhelmed more than ever as he sat up against the base of his tree that late afternoon, under a rust-colored, gloomy and sad sky.

Chapter Seven

TRUTH AND TRIBULATION

L ife on the Peterson Plantation was hard. The days spent in the field working long, slow-moving hours in either the sweltering hot sun or the merciless thunderstorms that often occurred with hardly any forewarning were physically draining, to say the least. Little regard was given to a field hand's well-being and regardless of age, gender or health, each laborer was expected and required to begin each work day by six a.m. and work all day until dusk. The lunch break, if one can consider such a break, happened only at the whelm of the miserable and often drunken field manager (who was a distant and very embittered distant cousin of Robert Peterson) and lasted only long enough for the field hands to hurriedly gulp down the food they kept stored in knapsacks tied around their waists or flung securely over their shoulders. The brevity of their lunch break was matched by the scarcity of the food in their sacks, which for most consisted of a dinner biscuit and a tiny portion of fruit preserve or apple or pear butter. On a good day, an extraordinarily good day, there would also be a scrap of meat, perhaps dried ham or day-old bacon. That short lunch break, along with swift and infrequent visits to the outer fields for personal relief, served as the only rest afforded to those burdened with the daily production of the crops that were the stronghold of the farming empire long held by the Peterson family.

The Peterson Plantation was renowned for its hearty, profitable output of cotton, corn, and okra each planting season and for years over, Robert Peterson claimed bragging rights for being the owner of the wealthiest and most efficiently run farmland in Chester County. Not only were his field hands incredibly useful, they were also a most peaceful bunch of overworked, overwhelmed, unpaid laborers and seldom did one hear of any kind of commotion or calamity amongst the residents of the Peterson Plantation. Unlike the countless stories of wife beatings, drunken brawls, and child neglect and abuse that were rampant occurrences amongst field workers on other plantations, few and far between were the disturbances set in motion by those who lived solely to work the Peterson fields.

Perhaps their civility was due to the proud and dignified nature of those who, in large majority, were descendants of slaves who had labored in the very same fields. Though their circumstances were oppressive, indeed, to them, the Peterson Plantation was still their homeland and the only home most of them and their forefathers and foremothers had ever known. And as burdensome as life was there, they all knew-for the most part, they all felt that, sadly enough, theirs was not the worst of plights, nor the most oppressive of circumstances. Maybe this sentiment drove their tendency to act sensibly and respectfully toward each other or maybe they were driven by their holding on to the faint hope that one day they might actually legally possess the small plot of the land that included their tiny cabins and small yards, if ever their debt to Robert Peterson was paid in full. Maybe that imagination governed their behavior night after night, at the close of the most tiring of days. Maybe, probably though, more than any other reason or factor, fatigue was the common motivator and denominator. Robert Peterson demanded so much daily output from his field hands, burdened them so heavily and worked them so vigorously each and every day, that they were just too tired to fight with, antagonize or abuse one another.

∞

On this particular night, both of Gabriel's parents were weary with that dogged tiredness. That day's labor had been especially grueling. The sun's brutal glare had shown no regard for their plight and had held its place high in a cloudless sky for what seemed like their longest day on earth, yet. Dusk had taken an especially long time to show up and when the whistle was finally blown, signaling the end of the work day, they both were entirely spent. Somehow, Rosalee and had pushed past her fatigue, in order to make supper. Her sagging shoulders and the deliberate movement of her arms and hands as she toiled over the hot, iron stove signified her exhaustion.

Usually John would not belabor his dear wife with any further need to further think or speak. That night, however, he could not afford her such grace. He had put the conversation off as long as he could and the time was now of the essence. The discussion, the probable debate and even the possible disagreement had plagued his mind for weeks and he was almost certain that she had been just as preoccupied, perhaps even more.

Since Benjamin's death, Rosalee seemed to live more inside her own mind than she did out loud and apparently. Although her constant grief did not sour her sweet nature, all who knew her felt the impact of her emotional absence. For years, she had been the gravity of the Quarters. She was a mother by the most natural of instincts and most of the girls and boys who grew up around her affectionately referred to her as "Mama Ro." She was a favorite among her peers, as well. Her male neighbors had often sought her out as a safe haven, a most reliable audience for their utterances of despair and worry, when they were too proud or too upset to confide in their own wives. She knew just how to listen and, then, how to reassure even the most anxious of men and they could always trust her to keep the woes they shared to herself. And to the other women of the Quarters, young and old, Rosalee was a big sister figure, a readily accessible shoulder to lean and cry on and a sharp, quick wit that offered the best advice on child-rearing blues and marital struggles.

She was the person people called on in the time of need. When someone died, the family sent for Rosalee. She knew what to say to the grieving family and she knew what to do, what necessary actions to take from the drawing of the deceased's last breath to the lowering of the body into the earth. When a baby was born or about to be born, the expecting family sent for her, not to serve as midwife, but to perform her well-established role as a counselor and guide to the new mother, one who could tell her what to do specifically for the baby just born. Because she had an insight into the uniqueness of each child she laid eyes upon, at first glance, Rosalee would speak of the new baby's nature and announce her expectation of his or her character. Almost always, in all matters, her wisdom was outweighed only by her kindness and generosity. She never seemed to mind being in such constant, high demand. As a matter of fact, such was her life's joy and, before Benjamin died, she was never too tired to answer the call of a neighbor in need.

The only cause that gave her more joy than helping others was the love and devotion she lavished upon her immediate family. As the only female in her home, Rosalee basked in the constant affection and attention from her faithful husband, her beloved sons, and her high-spirited brother in-law. They were the center of her life and her emotional state was influenced greatly by their comings and goings. She considered herself immensely blessed with the wholeness of a loving family, despite the frustrations of their dreary work conditions and the inadequacies of their meager resources. As far as Rosalee was concerned, she had what mattered most and life was worth living and experiencing to the fullest extent possible.

Since that early, dreadful morning when her husband walked through the back door of their cabin without her firstborn in tow, grief had taken up most of the space in her heart. The little room left was reserved for her husband and her one and only remaining child, Gabriel. Somehow, despite her uninterrupted heartache over the loss of Benjamin, the presence of Gabriel allowed her to still experience joy. Any laughter or slight smile upon her robust face, any sort of expression of glee at all, almost always could be attributed to something Gabriel said or did. Clearly, after Benjamin died, her concern and love for her youngest son was her motivation to carry on and to even allow herself to feel the happiness he brought into her life.

Before they lost Benjamin, John and Rosalee had a marriage that most couples, white or black, rich or poor, would envy. Simply put, they doted on each other. They moved through their lives in sync and with a deep devotion to their love. From the day he married Rosalee, John had basked in her love and desire for him. She was an outgoing woman and she never shied away from an opportunity to express her affection. Even during the height of the most cumbersome of planting seasons, they always stole away to have their "quiet" times with each other. Their passion grew, rather than faded, with the years and even though their neighbors relied on her for so much, John always knew that he was her priority and next to him, his sons, but when Benjamin died, death took the closeness they shared right along with the life of their precious, beautiful boy. His mind told him that such was the effect of such a harrowing loss and that his grief, as poignant as it was, paled in comparison to hers. In his heart, though, John anguished over the possibility that she somehow held him accountable for Benjamin's demise. Perhaps he had failed her by not being more stated with regard to Benjamin's tendency to work late into the night or, even more troubling, perhaps she resented the fact that he waited as long as he did to go and look for his son that fateful night. Whatever the matter in her mind, whatever the sentiment of her heart, John had lost more than his son when Benjamin's life was stolen away from the Loveman family. He had lost his union with his wife and they both moved about and around one another as shadows of their former selves. The only time they remotely emerged in true person was when Gabriel was present and even then they seemed to think and act separately.

In John's mind, the current matter before them was no exception. As much as the separateness pained him, his love for her out-matched any concern for his own well-being and, now that they only had Gabriel, he offered many a prayer of thankfulness that God had blessed them with two sons. As far as John was concerned there was no earthly reason good enough to take their only living child away from his wife, for doing so would surely deplete her of the little joy remaining in her heart. That thought alone was the driver for his mood on that sweltering evening, an evening made even hotter by the smallness of the cabin which was overcome with heat from the hot stove.

As Rosalee turned around to place the pot liquor and beans on the table, she was struck by the anguished expression on her husband's face.

"What's the matter John?" she asked.

"You know what the matter is." John said, quietly, with hardly any character of voice.

As she lowered their plate of supper to the table, Rosalee slid into chair opposite her husband, as he continued to talk, speaking very slowly and with hardly any show of emotion.

"You see him. You know how upset he is. And I know how upset he is. He don't want us to know. Don't want us to worry, I suppose. But he ain't got to say nothing, Rosalee. It's all over that boy and it's killing him. And that is killing me and you both. Only thing troubling me more is what I got to say to you now."

"And what is that Husband?"

Rosalee could not bring herself to look at him. She had no strength left and she did not know if she could handle her husband's response, regardless of the decision he had made, one way or the other.

When John spoke again, he spoke defiantly.

"Look at me. You gone have to look at me. Because I am going to need you to see why I am saying what I am going to say."

When Rosalee looked up, she had already begun to cry. The frustrated energy and the ever so thick tension that had replaced their love and passion since the day Benjamin died finally overwhelmed them both. And so, for the first time in the longest time, John got as close as he could with his wife by allowing himself to cry in front of her.

With a shaken voice and with tears streaming down his face, he looked his precious Rosalee squarely in her eyes and simply said, "He can't go."

Hearing such stark defiance in her husband's voice, Rosalee was instantly stricken by the gravity of his declaration. Rather than respond, she laid her head on the table, right beside the hot plate of food that neither of them had the stomach to consume and sobbed. Her cry was loud and piercing. With her wails returned the all too familiar disconnect between them and without uttering another word, John stood to his feet and walked away to leave Rosalee with her new-found sorrow. Though the sight and sound of his wife in pain shook him to the core, John had convinced himself that he had to break her heart in order to eventually save her heart. He had accepted he would never be able to bring Benjamin back. His heart was resigned to his inability to rewind the hateful clock that set the time that governed the saddest moment of his life and he knew he could not travel back in time and remake any of his decisions that horrible night Benjamin was lynched. There was no way he could go looking for Benjamin sooner, no way to protect his darling boy from his deadly fate and no way for him to have gotten to the death scene in time enough for him to stand between his child and the murdering mob and to offer up his life in his boy's stead. Day after day, John yearned for the chance to change the memory of that tragic summer's eve, all the while facing the cruel reality that life, chance and fate do not allow for instant or distant replay. John would never be able to undo what had already been done. He would never have the opportunity to be a better father to Benjamin or a better husband to Rosalee, more than likely. His best hope was that this outcome of would outweigh, outlast Rosalee's sadness and the disappointment caused by his decision to refuse Gabriel's departure from them. While he would never be able to bring Benjamin back to her and though he risked losing Gabriel's affection and respect because of his stance, at least keeping Gabriel close would ensure that his wife would have her only child, her only source of joy, near her every day for the rest of her life. At least, he was able to do that for her.

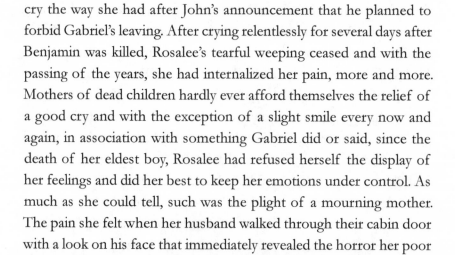

Many months had passed since Rosalee had allowed herself to cry the way she had after John's announcement that he planned to forbid Gabriel's leaving. After crying relentlessly for several days after Benjamin was killed, Rosalee's tearful weeping ceased and with the passing of the years, she had internalized her pain, more and more. Mothers of dead children hardly ever afford themselves the relief of a good cry and with the exception of a slight smile every now and again, in association with something Gabriel did or said, since the death of her eldest boy, Rosalee had refused herself the display of her feelings and did her best to keep her emotions under control. As much as she could tell, such was the plight of a mourning mother. The pain she felt when her husband walked through their cabin door with a look on his face that immediately revealed the horror her poor child endured before dying and the shrinkage of her husband's shoulders in a way that only death can induce- that pain was beyond the capacity of a human being's imagination. A pain so deep, so particular and definite can never be sufficiently described or expressed and every single happening in life reminds a mourning mother that she will bear that pain for the rest of her life. The only way Rosalee could tolerate moving through and about her remaining days was to remove herself as much as possible from the place in her heart that housed her grief. That place also held her happiness, her anger, her frustration, her fears, her hopes and all the emotions a woman is capable of experiencing. The only way Rosalee could exist in a world without her first born child was to move forward through life feeling as little of anything as possible. She existed rather than lived and as much as she had always loved her husband and her kinfolk, as much as caring for and taking care of her neighbors and friends had brought her joy and peace, after Benjamin died, Rosalee could barely feel anything for anyone, including herself. Any emotions she allowed herself at all were reserved almost strictly for her precious Gabriel.

The feat of caring for a living child after suffering the loss of another one is tricky, a very tricky, balancing act that became Rosalee's only effort, besides getting through her day-to-day struggle of working in the fields. Her grief over Benjamin and her love for Gabriel became dual endeavors and Rosalee had to connect with her feelings enough for Gabriel to know that her love for him was still in full effect. Still, if she felt too much, experienced life a little too extensively, the pain of losing Benjamin was reactivated to an almost deadly level, for fragile is the heart of a grieving mother. Only the love of another child keeps that mother's heart from breaking or bursting, entirely.

Shortly after Benjamin died, Rosalee had convinced herself that if she cried at all, she was likely to cry herself into an early grave and leave her living child to fare through the rest of his childhood motherless. A few days after her husband had come home without their firstborn child, to the surprise of many and to the worry of her husband and close kin, Rosalee stopped shedding tears for her darling Benjamin. Though she could not bring herself to explain her new manner of being, Rosalee knew that not crying and barely feeling her way through life had been her saving grace. Her love for her baby boy and her concern for his well-being had kept her from crying herself to death.

That evening's talk with John about Gabriel's future had awakened almost all of Rosalee's emotions, feelings that had lain dormant over the years since Benjamin was murdered. The night of John's announcement was a sleepless night for Rosalee. After tossing and turning, after weeping and wailing and wringing her hands the whole night through, she knew there were two things she had to do to save her second son's life. The first action could be accomplished with a visit to the schoolhouse and through one conversation with the teacher who had so much influence over her only living child. The other matter she had to handle herself and would take Rosalee a bit more courage, for the deed presented much more of a challenge to her heart and mind. She doubted if she would truly be able to succeed, but John's decision had triggered the ache that had gone unaddressed for far too long. Rosalee realized that she needed to cry for Benjamin and that night she accepted that she would have to learn how to cry for him possibly for the rest of her life without allowing her grief to overtake the rest of her emotions. To be the best mother she could be for both her sons, she would have to embrace life fully again. She also knew that in order to even begin to try and do so, she had to first make sure that what was best for Gabriel came to pass.

After overhearing John and Rosalee's conversation about Gabriel, David had thought long and hard about the best way to approach his brother to address the matter and weigh in as only he could. He knew what he wanted to say and what John needed to hear and he wanted to engage Rosalee's husband, Gabriel's father and his sibling in a manner that was certain to help be helpful in the resolution of matter in the best way for them all, including John. Life had hurt his older brother enough and with all that John had done for him over the years–sharing his home, looking after him in those early years when he was consumed with his own grief, allowing him to have such a close relationship with his nephews -for all of that, David owed his brother the unconditional love and support. He never wanted to do or say anything that would make John feel disrespected or misjudged. Still, after hearing what John said to Rosalee, he had to confront him. David knew that if ever there was a possibility of John living beyond his grief over Benjamin, any such possibility lie on the other side of the talk he had to have with his beloved older brother.

A few days after he had heard John speak his mind to Rosalee, David asked his brother to go for a walk with him. Their work day had come to a close and Rosalee was preparing dinner. They didn't have much time to eat and get a decent night's rest before they would have to be up and in the fields again. Given what he wanted to say, David didn't need much time. However, he did need to talk with his brother in private and a walk down the hill behind the Quarters seemed to be the ideal setting for the conversation he was set to have. Rosalee eyed them suspiciously, as John, without verbally responding, arose from the table in the middle of the cabin and followed David out the back door. When they were several feet away and could not be heard by Rosalee or anyone else, David wasted no time getting to the point. Right away, his first question made John aware that the two of them would be doing much more talking than walking.

"How come you don't sing no more?" David asked, as he locked eyes with his brother.

Just as much as John Loveman had not expected anyone to ever initiate a conversation with him about the most dreadful episode of his life, David did not expect his brother to actually respond to his question. They both knew, though, that David was purposely opening John's wound and they both knew that if there was anybody who could do so and actually illicit a response from John, that somebody was his trusted brother, not only because they had always been so close but also because John knew David could relate to his suffering. Years ago, when David's young wife died while giving birth to his son, who also did not survive the delivery, John had handled the burials for his grief-stricken younger brother and then moved him into the cabin with his own family, with the hope that his doing so would keep David safe and ease the despair and loneliness caused by the tragic and sudden loss.

Over the years, John had watched him recover and as his own sons grew, their Uncle David became more of a surrogate father who watched over Benjamin and Gabriel as if they were his own children. And though he could never thank his brother enough for sharing his home and family, David continually showed John his appreciation by doing whatever he could to support them all. There was nothing he wouldn't do for his brother and he would never do anything to deliberately harm him or cause him pain. And John knew that. He knew that his brother would never intentionally hurt him and even though the question David had just asked made him feel as though someone had punched him with a relentless force in the center of his chest cavity, John knew that his brother's query was an effort to open a very necessary dialogue between the two of them.

When a few moments had passed with no response from John, David took a deep breath and began to speak again.

"Well, I understand. I most certainly do. Yes sir, you got every right to never sing again, if such be your choosing. I reckon' there's no melody left in life after all you been through."

There was no need for David to elaborate any further. Both men knew that he was talking about Benjamin and the way John's oldest boy had died.

"But you still got Rosalee and you still got Gabriel." David stated.

Placing his hand on John's shoulder, gently shaking his brother as if he could maybe shake some sense into him, David pulled the one card that he believed would accomplish the trick of awakening his brother's senses.

"That's one wife and one boy more than I ever had."

David paused for a few seconds, to let his sorrowful reminder sink into John's psyche and then spoke aloud thoughts that had been lingering in his mind for the past several weeks, since the beginning of that summer.

"And that boy of yours is still as special as he was the day he was born and he needs you. Needs you now more than ever. Even if you can't bring yourself to sing no more, even if you don't ever again so much as hum a tune, you need to hold your head up and you need to straighten up your back. You being all sullen and broke down ain't no good for your wife or your boy. All you doing is holding on to your grief, dwelling on what happened, clinging to something you can't do nothing about."

Though he could see the stress in John's face as he spoke, David continued. He had to finish what he had started if there was any chance what he was saying would do any good and so he pressed even harder with his next declaration.

"The least you can do, John Loveman, is let loose that tight grip you got on the past, let go a little bit of all that pain you holding on to and come up out of that grave you dug for Benjamin almost five years ago now. You dug it for one son, not two, and you didn't dig that hole for yourself and it's time for you to start acting like you actually came home that morning. Otherwise, I'm mighty afraid that as much as you have already lost yourself, you going to lose Gabriel, as well. And then none of us will ever be any good at all, now will we?"

When John looked at David to respond, his eyes were filled with tears and when he spoke, his breath was shallow, his voice raspy.

"I don't want that. More than anything, I want Rosalee to be alright and I want my Gabriel to be safe. Lord knows I would give anything, my life even, for that to be."

David walked up as close as he could get to his brother and looked him squarely in his eyes, as he asked, "Would you give up your pain for them? You see, that pain you carrying around is so heavy, so sharp, ain't no way Rosalee don't feel it right along with her own. Even with you hardly ever talking to her or to anybody, for that matter. Don't matter that you don't talk about your hurt. You don't have to. You wrapped up in it. It's surrounding you. Poor Gabriel needs you, but, hell, he can't get to you, with all your pain standing between the two of you."

Placing both his hands on both of John's shoulders, David took his brother into his arms, as he decided that, with his own words, he would take the matter on entirely, that he would help his brother through the thicket of grief that had entangled the man since the night he lost his firstborn son. David knew he had to say, rather he had to raise the question to John no one else would dare to pose. Carefully, gently, David imposed on his brother in a way that was sure to create tension between the two men.

"What exactly did you come across that night when you went to look for Benjamin?" David asked, almost in a whisper.

John's head snapped up from David's shoulder, as he pushed himself back from his brother's embrace. Fury flooded through him as he responded.

"You know I don't talk about that. I never have and I never will."

David deepened his grip, refusing to release John from their embrace or his inquiry.

"Why not, John? Why haven't you talked about it?" David implored.

As the tears rolled down his cheeks, John shook his head in disapproval.

"Why in the world would you want me to? Why would you ask me such a thing?" he pleaded, his voice shaking with anger.

Relieved to see him feel something else other than sorrow, David sought to seize the opportunity to reach his dear old brother while grief was out of the way.

"I know I done made you mad! That's alright!" he exclaimed. "You can be mad but I still aim to ask you what happened. I want to know and you need to tell somebody. Long as you keep it to yourself, long as you hold it all in, you letting whatever you found that awful night take up all the space in your heart. Ain't no room left for Rosalee or Gabriel or me, speaking for myself, too. No room for nobody in there but yourself, you and your sorrow. I will do you one even better, Big Brother, 'cause I know you don't even realize it. But as long as you won't say what happened to him and just keep it to yourself, you ain't even got room for Benjamin in your heart. All you got room for in there is your self-pity and your pain."

What David was saying was too much to bear. John felt as if the scab had been ripped off of a sore, except the injury was to his soul and he wanted no more of the pain his brother's words were causing him to feel. He preferred much more to keep his grief hidden and buried, not up front and out in the open. John used all the energy he could gather to try and end the conversation. Desperately, he pleaded with David.

"You just need to hush your mouth. You don't know what you are talking about!"

"Oh." David paused and gazed up at the sky for a few seconds before he retorted. "Don't I know, John? Don't I know all about it?"

When John dropped his head in shame for saying anything to suggest that David had not suffered his own tragic loss, the younger of the two brothers took advantage of the chance to reconnect with his mentor, his best friend and closest kin.

"Loss. Pain. Sadness. It's all the same, no matter what the cause. I know how you feel. I know the heartbreak that death brings. And I know that if you hadn't shared my grief with me, if you hadn't taken care of me, you and Rosalee, the way you did, I would have shriveled up and died a long time ago. Even if this body of mine was still alive, had it not been for the way you have been here for me, I would be just a shell of a man walking around, feeling nothing and just barely existing. The same shell of a man you done become these past few years. I done sat back and watched long enough. Now it's time for me to help you the way you helped me way back when I was the one needing to be saved from myself."

As David spoke, John's heart broke all over again and he felt as anguished and as helpless as he had the moment he had found Benjamin's body in the woods that cold, bitter night, so many summers ago.

"How can you help me, David? How can anybody help me? Benjamin is gone. Nothing is going to bring him back." he cried, as he shifted his weight and collapsed into his baby brother's arms.

As he responded, David slowly rocked his brother, holding him in an embrace that had been long in the waiting, one they both had needed since the day John came home without Benjamin. David's grip and his next words consoled them both and resealed their brotherly bond.

"I can help you by reminding you that you still got one son left. At least you still have a child and you have a wife, a lovely soul of a woman and they both love and need you. I can help by just sitting here and listening as you tell me what happened to your other boy and to you that God-forsaken night. I want to know and you need to tell me. That way, from now on, you will know that you have somebody who understands why you so quiet, why you never sing no more. You'll have somebody who will know just how to help you get along better through your grief. You did it for me. Now let me do it for you."

And with that John and David's brotherhood reached its highest peak. In that moment, their bond tightened and became stronger than ever and for the first time, John Loveman relayed the details of the night he found Benjamin's dead body. What he described was much more horrible than David had ever imagined and by the time John shared how he sang as he covered his son's charred remains with dirt, both men cried profusely. It was a good cry, the kind of weeping that purges and cleanses one's soul, and when they collected their wits and walked back toward the cabin that they called home, John felt better than he had since Benjamin died. The weight of his grief over his firstborn had not been lifted but it had been redistributed and was now shared with his brother in a way that made life going forward seem more bearable. For the first time since he buried his beautiful boy alone in those dreary, death-bearing, dark woods, John Loveman felt alive.

Chapter Eight

RESIGNATION AND REDEMPTION

The births and deaths of the colored population of the Peterson Plantation were only officially recognized in the accounting books that kept track of Robert Peterson's financial assets and liabilities. As far as he was concerned there was no need to otherwise acknowledge the existence of those he considered to be unworthy of human regard. Until a child was old enough to work in the fields or assist in the upkeep of his mansion and immaculate grounds, a newborn baby was only a projected benefit that, in the meanwhile, slowed down production while the mother recuperated from the delivery. The death of a laborer was merely a nuisance. As far as Robert Peterson was concerned, any field hand thoughtless and thankless enough to die wasn't worthy of a decent burial and not even the colored preacher man would dare to suggest that the deceased's family and friends be granted time out of the field to memorialize their fallen loved one. Besides, most of the Quarters community felt that they best honored the dead by putting them away as soon as the day's labor ended, if they died in the daytime. Those who passed away at night were given an abbreviated version of the evening burial ceremony and were laid to rest quickly between breakfast, which was shortened by ten minutes, and the onset of the workday. The immediate family of the deceased would each be acknowledged by name by a neighbor designated by the family to assist with the ceremony, who also would then lead the gathered crowd in a hymn. The Preacher Man would then speak about the best qualities of the man or woman laid out before them, noting particularly anything that made him or her special and distinctive amongst the residents of the Quarters. Somehow, as a man of God, he managed to find something good or kind to say about anyone who suffered the plight of farming on the Peterson Plantation. Even still, the most notable of lives were summarized in two to three minutes and the plainer the life, the shorter the speech. The closing prayer for all was the same. "Dear Lord, neighbor is dead now and a field hand, no more. If neighbor be Your child, Lord, please give him some joy and peace, for neighbor hardly had any such a thing on this here side. And if neighbor wasn't a true child of God, and only You know that, Lord, have mercy on neighbor, anyway, and at least give him rest for never was such a pleasure while down here on earth. Amen."

With that, the body that had been wrapped in a sackcloth that was tightly tied at both ends. was placed in a shallow at the very edge of the living quarters, which was marked by the largest rock a loved one could find. At any given time, one could walk past the make-shift graveyard and note easily those who had family members who placed an importance on paying the highest respect to those who had preceded them in death by continuing to place large, distinctive rocks on the graves of their loved ones past. The placement of multiple markers meant that in whatever spare time they had, which was extremely little, the deceased's family members were replacing the rocks that were always up for grabs whenever another neighbor passed away. Whenever a marker went missing, usually, no offense was taken. Most everyone in the Quarters understood how little time was available for burial and accepted that a mourner would look for a large rock in the place one was most likely to be found. That graves for field hands of the Peterson Plantation would probably go unmarked or bear a marking for a very short while was their reality and another reminder of how little value was placed on their lives.

∞

Before Eli passed away, Gabriel had only thought about how his decision would impact him and his family and, possibly, Ella and her family, but his next door neighbor's death had jolted him to the core, blindsided him with a realization of how in the Quarters, everybody's lives were intertwined. Knowing that Eli had died at the hands of Robert Peterson had shaken Gabriel in the place that had been dormant since a day or so after Benjamin had been killed. As a reminder of the heaviness of Robert Peterson's hand, Eli had served as yet another sacrificial lamb offered up as a statement, an instruction to Gabriel. "Don't even think about it or this is what you will get." The "it" was not just leaving and prevailing by pursuing an education and a life far away from the Peterson Plantation. Piercingly the extent of the "it" was that, as far as Robert Peterson and men like him earnestly believed, the Gabriels, the Elis and the Benjamins of the world should accept that they worked every day of their lives for the sole sake of fattening the pockets of white men and should never dare to imagine more than a meager existence for themselves. To dare to migrate toward a life that indicated a value remotely equivalent of that of a white man was to place his life and the lives of those he loved at an extreme risk.

By applying for admission to college and by receiving both the acceptance and the partial scholarship, Gabriel had signaled to Robert Peterson that he was on the move and, by beating Eli, Robert Peterson had sent a clear message to Gabriel that anyone associated with Gabriel was in danger and at any given time, Robert Peterson stood ready to remind them all that a nigger's life was purposeful only to the extent that he decided it was.

Robert Peterson had fully intended the end result of Eli's beating, for he had stood close by after commanding his only white employee to apply the whip and spare no mercy to the elderly field hand. Even after several minutes of nonstop strikes across Eli's back and despite the poor's man's tormented pleas for relief and his begging for forgiveness for whatever wrongful act he committed, Robert Peterson had refused to issue an order to stop the punishment. With a hint of amusement in his voice, he had encouraged strike after strike with a slow nod of his head and an insistent drawl of his "Uh huh. Yeah. Keep it going."

The beating lasted well over ten minutes and was more than even the healthiest person could endure. When it was over, the old man's entire upper torso was torn apart, his clothes ripped and bloodied and his already weakened body was, without a doubt, injured beyond repair. In his determination to get as far away from the man who so cruelly ordered his fate, Eli had apparently crawled part of the way back down the dusty lane, trying his best to make it home and to not die anywhere near the main house. He did not want the last person to see him alive to be Robert Peterson. He did not want to die like a mere pet or farm animal and, only to then be treated like any other carcass in need of discarding. Between the dirt and the dust, his mangled flesh, the ragged clothing and the blood, by the time Eli made it to the edge of the Quarters, one could barely see the entirety of his form and only his face was recognizable.

Gabriel saw his old friend alive only once after that awful afternoon when he found Eli drenched in sweat and blood, lying listlessly on the makeshift porch to his cabin. After discovering his neighbor beaten nearly to the point of death and after listening to several other neighbors and friends speculate as to why the poor old man had undergone such a blistering attack, the next day, Gabriel had gone into his Eli's tiny cabin and sat beside his sick bed. The sight of Eli was more than horrifying than the day before. What happened to him was maddening and incomprehensible. Why another man would mistreat another man in such a demoralizing and demeaning manner was baffling and infuriating, except Gabriel knew how the kind of beating Eli suffered was always possible on the Peterson Plantation. He knew that Robert Peterson's cruelty towards others was an accepted reality that hardly anyone would ever seek to criticize, let alone prosecute. The reason why he did the things he did to the people he did them to was simple. To him, people of color were and always stood to be niggers and niggers were beings that were only slightly more valuable than common farm animals and far less worthy than the most pathetically poor white people. Their human value was almost nonexistent in the minds of Robert Peterson, his family, friends and colleagues and he could treat a nigger, any nigger, as he so pleased or deemed necessary. Eli's fate had occurred because, socially, the extensive beating of an old nigger was of no offense to the society to which Robert Peterson belonged and that he desired to commit the act was the only reason that was necessary for the beating to take place. As Gabriel sat beside his dying neighbor, the day after he had received what was supposed to be the best news of his life, he was tormented knowing Eli's plight was not due simply because of Robert Peterson's usual evil notion. Gabriel knew the arrival of the letter and Eli's presence at the Peterson mansion at the most ill-fated of times was why the old man had been subjected to the beatdown that eventually led to his death.

As Gabriel sat listening intensely to Eli's labored breathing and watching the pain ripple through his broken body, he did his best to tell Eli how very sorry he was for what happened to him. Although, deep down, Gabriel wanted Eli's forgiveness, at the same time, he felt so guilty and undeserving, he was prepared to accept Eli's rejection of his apology. When he realized that the poor man was too weak to answer him one way or the other, Gabriel took their time alone to promise Eli he would stay by his side as much as possible and forego everything except his required field work, even his studies and even his time with Ella, to assist with Eli's recovery. When his promise was met with more silence, Gabriel figured the old man had drifted off to sleep and saying anything else would be useless. As he stood and turned to go, Eli, who had been awake all along, mustered all of his remaining strength to grab ahold of Gabriel's shirt sleeve. Lifting his head modestly to look into the eyes of the young man he had known since he was born, Eli then spoke what would turn out to be his last words in life when he whispered to Gabriel to depart from his dying bed and never return.

"Keep to yourself boy. Keep away from me and keep yourself alive," he insisted from the bed that held him for weeks before he took his last breath. Everyone who loved and cared for Eli, including Gabriel, was relieved when the old man finally escaped his suffering and died.

Oddly enough, on the morning of Eli's burial, as he walked back from the brief and hasty funeral, Gabriel, felt deeply saddened and infuriated by the cause of Eli's death. After he had received his forgiveness and his instructions from the dying man, in obedience, Gabriel had kept his distance. His family and other neighbors thought that he had done so because seeing Eli was so painfully mindful of what Benjamin must have endured the night he died. Only Gabriel, himself, knew exactly why Eli had been subjected to such a wretched demise and so his grief over his favorite neighbor's death was intensified by the secrecy of his acceptance letter, the dreadful yet remarkable sheet of paper that could bring so much freedom but that so far had only brought more pain and sorrow into his life.

Maybe if Eli had been able to get back on his feet or maybe even if he had died a few more weeks later, Gabriel would not have felt so responsible for what had happened. Walking back from Eli's shallow grave, he felt all the more weary, as he could not help but to think that acting on the letter simply was not worth the risk of anyone else suffering the same plight that had placed Eli in the ground. The mere imagination of any of his loved ones undergoing such an attack stole his breath and when he unknowingly sucked air between his teeth, he caught the attention of his Mother, who turned and looked his way.

Rosalee knew Gabriel was especially grieving Eli. The air and the mood surrounding them as they walked up the hill back toward their cabin felt as thick as mud. Her maternal instinct had also cued her in on the fact that her boy was suffering beyond the typical sadness of losing an old friend. Even beyond the tragic circumstances of Eli's death, something else was the matter. Rosalee knew her son was troubled and had been so for weeks. She could feel the weight of his conflict, even if he hadn't said a word to her about his dilemma. She had a connection to her youngest child that was mystical and that had preceded his birth. In Rosalee's mind, Gabriel was actually seven, maybe eight, children all shaped and molded into one glorious genius of a human being and she also felt that nobody, not even her husband, really understood that about her boy wonder. Deep in her heart, though, Rosalee had long suspected that as he grew from boy to man, Gabriel had begun to understand just why he was so special. Better yet, even if he did not completely comprehend the mystique of his conception and birth, he had begun to experience the totality of his existence.

Rosalee had known from the day he entered into the world that he would come to know himself entirely and she had always known that his awareness of himself would be overwhelming and, perhaps, burdensome. That Gabriel had Benjamin for a big brother, an earthly guardian had served as Rosalee's joy and comfort. The two of them were coupled in a most celestial kind of way and they were her glory, indeed, her heaven on Earth. Along with her love for John and her care for David, Rosalee bore the life of a sharecropper as happily as anyone cursed with such a circumstance could ever bear. The generosity of her spirit compelled her to share her joy, to spread that cheer as much as she could to others and she had been the most selfless of souls. When Benjamin died, when her firstborn was not just killed but lynched and maimed beyond her being able to place eyes upon him in his restful state, Rosalee felt as though she not only had lost her oldest child, but she also had lost that force field of love, trust and protection that existed between Benjamin and Gabriel. When she mourned so achingly for Benjamin, day after day, week after week, month after month and all the years that had passed since he had been taken from her, she had mourned deeply for Gabriel, as well. Because he no longer had Benjamin with him to shield and shelter him, Gabriel, the prodigy, the one that was born equipped with a mind and spirit that could change the world, was in danger himself of not surviving the challenges of life on the Peterson Plantation.

Walking alongside Gabriel with all of the thoughts of Eli and Benjamin running through her mind, Rosalee suddenly and starkly realized how absolutely selfish she had been. Something about the heaviness of the mood between the two of them, something about the way in which Gabriel was holding his face and posturing his body as he trod up the hill, something about the way they had unintentionally walked away together from everyone else heading back from Eli's final rites and the sharpness in which he had just drawn breath, awakened Rosalee to the fullness of her absenteeism from her son over the past five years.

She had been so preoccupied with mourning Benjamin, so focused on the breaking of her own heart that she had neglected Gabriel when he needed her most. Because each and every tear she shed for Benjamin contained every ounce of her own strength, Rosalee had not protected her boy genius, when protection was most required.

Along her way up that steep and grassy hill, back to a day of staunching labor and the reality that folks like her were not afforded the dignity of time to properly grieve and mourn loved ones lost, Rosalee turned and looked at her son and, right then and there, realized the impact of her grief. Given her realization, being who she was, understanding God the way she did, she forgave herself and, in seconds, reclaimed her motherhood. Gabriel needed her and she knew she had no time to waste. Rosalee knew she had to seize the moment and have a very necessary conversation with Gabriel, while the two of them were alone.

"You mighty quiet, Son." she began.

"Aren't I always?" he asked. Gabriels' reply was curt, although his tone, as usual, was mannerable.

"I suppose. But you know you got different ways of being quiet. There's you being quiet 'cause such is your natural way and then there's this. You being quiet 'cause so much is on your mind, so much you need to say, you don't know where to begin and so you say nothing. Not many people know that about you. But I'm your Momma. I know."

"I'm alright, Momma."

The last thing Gabriel wanted to do was have a heavy conversation with his mother. They were an honest family. Lies had never come between them and Gabriel was determined that they never would. He was also afraid that if he talked to her about anything that morning, he would wind up telling her everything and so he continued walking and said nothing else.

A few steps later, his mother spoke again, her words quickening as her breath became short as they made their way up the steep hill. There was no such thing as an excuse for tardiness and all the laborers knew to get in place before the field manager arrived or else they would suffer the humiliation and pain of a beating for being late.

"Son, it's a shame what happened to Eli. Just a sin and a shame but I don't want you to trouble yourself over it too much. Ain't nothing we can do for him now and you getting all worked up over it won't be no help to none of us."

"Yes Ma'am," Gabriel replied, his voice filled with acknowledgment and respect.

"'Sides that, he in a better place, far better than the rest of us."

"Yes Ma'am," said Gabriel, conceding to his Mother's need to speak her mind.

"You got anything else you want to say 'sides "yes ma'am?" Rosalee asked with a huff.

Anticipating his response, Rosalee spoke over his next response and engaged her son in a way that was long overdue, speaking to him with a candor that she had never before displayed, at first because she didn't have to and then, after everything that had happened to Benjamin, because she did not have the strength. That morning, though, after burying Eli and while climbing the hill back from their neighbors new grave, Rosalee had gained her strength, at least enough to take care of her boy. And so she opened her heart and her mouth in order to help her living child.

"Well, I got something else I want to say, something I been wanting to say and just ain't had the nerve to say it. Now that I got you to myself for a bit, I ain't got much time to say it, but I need to tell you what's on my mind."

Rosalee paused, taking a few seconds to catch her breath which had grown a bit short as she and Gabriel had walked uphill the last couple of minutes. As she started to speak again, tears welled in her eyes and she found herself overcome with emotion.

"Son. My darling, darling son. I am so sorry."

Seeing her state and wanting desperately to not see her upset for any reason, Gabriel responded quickly.

"Momma, you have no reason to feel or say you sorry. Nobody faults you for how you feel, everybody knows that Benjamin, well, he was the best thing that ever happened to all of us. You have no cause to say you sorry, not to me, Momma, not to anyone."

"Yes I do." Rosalee was adamant as she cut him short and continued. "Yes I do," she repeated. Then drawing a long breath, she spoke her mind as truthfully, as clearly as she could.

"I been away from you. Truth is, since Benjamin died, I been away from everybody. But more than anyone and in the worst of ways, Baby, I been away from you. I ain't got no excuse for it. Even my heartache for your brother, even the horror of it all ain't no excuse

102

for a mother abandoning her child and that's what I done did. I done left you to yourself it seems or at best, left you to that teacher of yours. She care for you. I know that. I don't fret that at all. Never did. But you ain't her child. You mine and I shoulda been here for you."

By this time, Rosalee was crying as much as she was talking and the sight and sound of her despair was almost more than Gabriel could handle. Her sorrow of any kind, for any reason, was one of the biggest challenges to a decision on his part to leave.Since he wasn't quite ready to make his decision, he really didn't want the weight of her words and her weariness on his mind.

"Momma," he interrupted. "There is no need for you to carry on this way. I know Eli passing away has upset you. I know it reminds you of Benjamin…"

Hearing Gabriel say his brother's name aloud somewhat startled Rosalee and she reached out, grabbing ahold of her son's shoulder as she steadied her walk.Turning his body to face her, Rosalee looked as deeply as she could into Gabriel's eyes.

"Hold on, Son, and hush up, now. I need you to let me have my say," she all but pleaded.

Pausing and taking Gabriel's chin into her hand and gazing upon his face as closely as she could, Rosalee spoke to her son as if the moment was her last chance to ever speak with him. She had never had such an opportunity with Benjamin and losing him the way she did had stolen so much. She refused to lose her chance with Gabriel and so she collected herself as much as she could and continued.

"Benjamin." she said, in barely above a whisper. Then, speaking a little louder, Rosalee poured her heart out.

"Seems to me I haven't heard you say your brother's name in the longest time, maybe not since that day, huh? I suppose that's my fault. The way I been carrying on I suppose you hadn't felt like it was right or safe to talk about him, let alone say his name. I know it seem like I been lost inside my grief for Benjamin. And so I have. It's true. I ain't been able to do much but get through the days, grieving all the while. Best I can explain is I lost my way, Son. You see, your Brother wasn't the first child the Lord saw fit to take from me. There was children between the two of you that never got a chance to so much as see the light of one day on Earth. Still I loved each and every one I carried. Happened so many times, I grew strong and figured the Lord was having his way with me and at the same time saving His angels from having to live this pitiful life, from having to walk such a miserable journey on their way back to him. Least that's what I told myself. That and plus I was 'specially blessed with the likes of Benjamin. And so I didn't much grieve them after the first couple of times. I learned how to get on about my way whenever it happened. Learned how to be joyful even if I couldn't be happy. And then you came. And it all made sense."

As she spoke, something deep inside of Rosalee shifted and with each word, she felt her heart growing lighter and lighter. As she gave her truth to Gabriel, she gained more and more strength and for the first time in years, she felt in touch with herself. The spark gave her the courage to speak her mind and Gabriel noticed a bit of a glimmer in her eyes. They weren't sparkling but they were brighter than they had been in the five years since Benjamin died. He listened without so much as uttering a sound, forgetting all of his troubles and worries and losing himself inside the safety of his beloved mother's voice.

He had heard about her child-bearing trials from others but hearing her speak of it awakened an awareness of himself that, though dormant, had always dwelled in the back of his mind, a cosmic sense of being more than just himself, a feeling as if he existed as a representative of others that he did not know, perhaps would never know. Rosalee had always been able to read Gabriel's mind and so she was not alarmed when, without saying a word, with just the tilt of his head and the straightening of his back, he let her know just how much he understood what she was saying, that she could go on without having to explain what they both understood about her miscarriages. Just as he conjured the thought, his mother aligned the rest of what she had to say to him her along the same.

"You is everyone of them others all wrapped in one and then some. Soon as I saw you, soon as everybody saw you, it was understood. You, Gabriel, you something else. You like magic and mystery and love and power. It's like God's holy hand touched you so that every other time I carried and lost was worth the bearing if it meant that's how you were to come to be. Me, your Daddy, your Uncle, all the folks of the Quarters and all around, we knew that about you. But Benjamin, well Benjamin, he knew better than anybody. He understood it. Knew just how to handle it and exactly how to handle you, so I didn't worry about you being so gifted. I used to chuckle when I would look at the two of you together. I remember one day though, I had a thought of how Jesus had John the Baptist and so you had Benjamin. I wasn't meaning no blaspheme, now. The Lord knows that. I just knew that was how much Benjamin knew who you were born to be, what was meant for you in this world. While he was here, Lord blessed me with heaven on Earth, 'tween the two of you and your Daddy. And then hell came, the day those evil men took him from me."

Rosalee seemed sad again, but only for a few seconds. She shook her head as she shook off the sadness in order to finish what she had to say to Gabriel. What she conveyed to him that morning stood to change his life. She hoped with all her heart that it would.

Her tone was confident as she closed her conversation.

"But I need you to know, all my heartache, all the tears I have cried haven't been just for Benjamin. I been caught up in grief and fear. As soon as I knew he was lost to me for good, I couldn't get away from the thought that I was gonna lose you, too. That they took him first 'cause they knew that long as he was around he would keep you safe. I haven't much been able to handle my own thoughts. Between the grief and the fear, I just been hardly living at all, let alone being a wife and a mother, just wastin' my life away, I suppose. But really, Gabriel, there is no such a thing as a wasted life, no matter how rough things get or may be. Family, friends like Eli, well that's what keeps us going. Even with my child gone, he still keeps me going. Out there in that field all day, I think of him. I see him in everything I do and it gets me through."

Rosalee realized how what she said may have left Gabriel feeling lacking. Nothing was farther from the truth.

"I think about you too, Gabriel. More than you know. More than I can say, Son."

Hearing the voices of the other mourners, Rosalee released Gabriel and began walking, heading back to their cabin which was only a few feet away. Determined to say all she wanted to convey to her baby boy, she began to speak with a more hurried pace.

"Look Son. I'm better now. I don't expect I will ever be the same as I was 'fore everything happened. But I done decided to come out that hell them white folks put me in. Somehow, what happened to Eli has reminded me of two things. One, the Lovemans ain't so special as to escape the trials of any colored man or woman. What happened to Benjamin done happened to colored boys time and time again. Long as white men chose to mark their journeys with evildoing, ours will be marked with the bearing of their ways. Two, me being afraid for you won't stop that from happening. But it will stop me from being your rightful mother and loving you and guiding you the way I'm supposed to."

Rosalee wanted Gabriel to focus on every single word she had left to say. If they never spoke in this manner, again, if they went the rest of their lives without having a like conversation, she wanted her final words to resonate in a way that he would be sure to never forget what she so desperately wanted him to know, what only she could tell and teach him.

"I say all of this to say, Son. When it comes to Benjamin, I can't help that I'm sad but from now on, I'm gonna try not to act as sad and do my best to not be as sad. And something else you need to know and I mean this. More than anything I have said this morning, I mean this most of all. Gabriel, you are the best thing. If he was here, Benjamin would tell you that himself 'cause you was the best thing that ever happened to him. Part of what they took from me was, I don't get to watch him love you. You, Gabriel Loveman are the best thing that has happened to us all. I know I haven't acted like it. I haven't made you feel that way and I know it's probably always been hard for you to feel that way especially when Benjamin was here. He was so much of everything we all wanted to be. But more than anything when I miss him and when I cry, I miss the way he looked at you and I miss the way he loved you and I know you don't have that now that he is gone. On top of that, 'cause of my grief, I guess you lost me too. I know your daddy and your uncle been there for you, at least trying their best to so be, but I haven't been able to try but I'm telling you from now on, from this day forward, I'm gonna do more than try. I am going to be here. For you, Gabriel, I am here now. So hear me when I say this. Listen good, 'cause I will only say it this one time."

Rosalee drew another deep breath and let out a sigh that seemed filled with relief and conviction. She smiled as she spoke, not a big smile, but a hint of the one that had gone hidden behind her sorrow. Suddenly, Gabriel could hear a bit of joy in her voice as she finally counseled him.

"No matter what you do in this life, always know that your mother understands exactly who you are and why you choose to do what you do. You are the best thing that ever happened to me and for me and that's enough for me. I can be at peace, even have some joy long as I know that you at peace with who you are, with how God made you to be and that you have that peace wherever you are. Here with us all your days or…"

And that was the last of her say. Before she could finish, Gabriel and Rosalee noticed that John and David were only a few steps away and within range of hearing their conversation, so instead of completing her last sentence, Rosalee simply looked at her boy again in his eyes and gave him a quick, but ever so loving, nod of her head. There was no more time for talk, only the day's work to be done and decisions to be made.

∞

On her way to the schoolhouse Rosalee was overcome by the gravity of her decision. For so many reasons, she knew that what she was about to do was well beyond anything she had ever imagined herself doing. For one, her next conversation could get her and her whole family killed. If not that, her next move stood to destroy Gabriel's relationship with the teacher he loved so dearly. Not only that, though, for the first time ever, since the day she had laid eyes on John Loveman, the man she loved and trusted and obeyed with all her heart and might, for the first time ever, she was going to defy her husband and disobey his command. After her talk with Gabriel earlier that day, after seeing, hearing and feeling the conflict that was tearing her youngest child up inside, Rosalee's decision had been confirmed. As nervous as she was, for the first time since Benjamin died, she also felt alive, almost whole.

Truth be told, the moment her husband had walked through the door alone the morning after Benjamin's murder, the second she had looked into John's reddened eyes and as soon as she heard the dread in his voice as he spoke of what had happened to her darling boy, Rosalee had plunged into a grief that many were sure would eventually kill her. Losing her son and all the more, never having the chance to say goodbye, if only to his cold corpse, had ripped her heart into pieces. The initial stinging ache of the fracture had evolved into a dull and consistent pain over the years, one that somehow allowed Rosalee to get back on her feet for the sake of the field work that she had no choice but to return to and back into the kitchen to prepare the meals that were necessary for her family's vitality. That was all her grief allowed her to manage. All else that she ever did or participated in was lost along with her beautiful Benjamin. From the day of his death, Rosalee had taken on the bitter effort of existing in an almost zombie-like state. She had never intended to do so but like any parent who suffers the most unnatural of occurrences life can bring, Rosalee had not known how to pay homage to her love for her lost child and at the same time be zealous in the living of the rest of her life. Those who knew her well figured that the death of Benjamin, along with all the other unborn and stillborn babies, had simply been too much and so they excused and forgave her demeanor. No one pushed her to do better, to be better, for everyone felt strongly that Rosalee was coping as best as she could. Knowing his wife the way he did, knowing how faithful and trusting she was in God's will, John knew that Rosalee's state of being after they lost Benjamin was purposeful on her part and he had accepted that his happy marriage, his thriving family and any joy he ever was blessed to experience had died right along with his first born. As much as it pained him, John knew that the day he returned to their rugged cabin without their oldest boy in tow, he had all but lost Rosalee, as well. She had taken to the bed for days and only the threat of the field manager beating her and ousting them from their home had aroused her. Folks in the field covered her required daily output until she was able to manage enough energy to do her work and then, a few months later, she had assured the other women of the Quarters that she could resume cooking for her family. That had been the extent of Rosalee's return to herself. Gone from her was the robust laughter as she watched babies enter the world. Gone were the words of wisdom she so readily spoke whenever a neighbor came to her bearing trouble or trial. Gone away was the most cheerful of matriarchs, the woman who relished in each and every task that had anything to do with the raising of her sons and the guiding of any child of the Quarters. Gone was the friend and confidant that her brother-in-law had come to rely on as a source of comfort and strength that kept him from going through life as a sad soul and gone was John's lover, his life partner, the one who would read his mind and sometimes resituate his thoughts with nothing more than a quick turn of her head and a release of a smile that warmed his heart and soul.

For years, Rosalee had barely been herself, whenever she was herself at all. In a cryptic coincidence, Eli's death had given birth to the Rosalee of old, for the way he died had awakened some of the same emotions she felt the morning she learned of Benjamin's bitter end. Those feelings were met with her current day's worry over Gabriel and her soul had been stirred. She had been awakened at heart and had decided to live. Ironically, the taking back of her life would first start with her placing herself in danger for the sake of her one living son.

∞

As Rosalee made her way down the path to the schoolhouse, she could not help but notice the beauty of the day. The heat of the day's sun was undeniable, however, unlike most every other summer day, the heat this particular eve was not unbearable. In fact, Rosalee felt rather cloaked in the warmth, as if an invisible blanket was wrapped around her arms and shoulders as she headed toward the tiny school where her youngest child spent so much of his free time. Not until she was right upon the door entry did Rosalee realize that she had actually never stepped foot inside the schoolhouse. This was her first visit and, if she was successful, she figured her first attendance would also be her last.

"Evening Martha."

From the way she addressed her, by the election to refrain from the use of a title of respect or designation, Martha instantly knew Rosalee was there to discuss matters that would not allow for any pretense and that had to occur between the two of them without any reservation. Gazing up from the papers she was reviewing, Martha braced herself and then slightly bent her head in invitation for Rosalee to come inside. When she spoke, she did her very best to do so with as welcoming a tone as possible.

"Good evening, Rosalee. Come in and have a seat, why don't you?"

Rosalee's reply was cloaked in a subtle indignation. "I don't want to sit. I would rather stand, if you don't mind, please Ma'am."

"Well, of course, Rosalee….whatever you like."

Martha had always tried to show the utmost respect and deference to Gabriel's mother. As much as she valued and enjoyed every moment she spent teaching and interacting with the boy genius, she recognized the fact that the time spent with him took time away from his family. After his older brother was killed, Martha was even more sensitive to Rosalee's claim on Gabriel and she never wanted to position herself in a way that threatened or undermined either of the boy's parents. Martha especially did not want to lend to the ideology that most southern white people exuded in their dismissal and disregard of the sanctity of colored people's family ties. Although she had long ceased any effort to befriend the Lovemans, Martha's love for Gabriel extended to his family and especially to his mother.

For years, Martha had observed the comings and goings of Rosalee Loveman. She was astounded at how a woman living in and subjected to such miserable circumstances could be so openly joyful and compassionate. Martha would often witness or learn of some loving gesture by Rosalee or notice her engaged with her husband and her boys and then find herself wondering if she would have been that kind of wife and mother, if she herself had taken the other path life had once offered. When Gabriel's big brother was senselessly murdered, Martha could not help but stand in awe of the woman's ability to even go on living. Like everyone else who knew Rosalee, she did have to admit, though, that the woman she knew before Benjamin died was much different from the Rosalee standing in front of her. The only apparent remnant of the former Rosalee was the poor woman's love for her only living son, Gabriel.

No matter how much Rosalee grieved for her lost child, she remained defiant in her care and protection over her youngest boy. Undoubtedly, she would do anything out of her love for Gabriel. Despite the cloak of sadness that seemed to cover her from head to toe without interruption, everyone knew that Rosalee still would go to the end of the earth and back again for Gabriel. She had demonstrated just that by making her way down to the end of the path to the Martha's schoolhouse in order to accomplish the unspeakable act of confronting a white woman, all the while knowing that her doing so could lead to her demise, given the times in which she lived. For Rosalee, the possible outcome of the confrontation was worth the risk of her life and she was determined to have a conversation with her boy's teacher, a verbal exchange that perhaps stood to change Gabriel's life and the lives of just about everyone he knew and loved, including his devoted teacher and mentor.

Martha tried to ease the obvious tension that filled the room by maintaining the most friendly demeanor as she could display without coming across as patronizing. The last thing she wanted to do was insult the woman she admired so very much.

"How are you today, Rosalee?" Martha asked.

Rosalee looked straight into Martha's eyes and replied plainly, profoundly.

"I am the same as I am every day, Ms. Martha. I'm tired."

At first Martha was a bit taken aback by her visitor's response. She hadn't expected Rosalee to be so direct, so curt. Within seconds, though, Martha remembered exactly why she had no reason and certainly no right to be offended. The woman standing in the doorway looked tired, as exhaustion was her typical state of being. Working the cruel and unrelenting fields of any farm was exhaustive work. Being a laborer on the Peterson Plantation, day after day, year after year, was sheer agony. Rosalee also had the added burden of grief to drain any tiny bit of energy she had left after her workday ended. As a matter of fact, Rosalee had come to appreciate the heat, the sweat, even the aches and pains that came along with each day in the field. Her mind's preoccupation with the discomfort of her work was much preferred over her thoughts being set on the longing for Benjamin. Every day, once the whistle was blown, bringing her labor to an end and taking Rosalee back to the tiny shack she called home- once she no longer had to focus on working as much and as hard and fast as she could, Rosalee's thoughts would immediately turn to the sharp ache that lingered in the deepest crevices of her heart. Her nights brought little rest and hardly any relief from her daily struggles. Indeed, Rosalee Loveman was entitled to the indignation of her tiredness and Martha was charged with the humility of creating and maintaining the pleasantry of their interaction, if such a pleasantry was to exist between the two of them.

With a hint of cheer, she asked, "Well, what brings you by this evening, Rosalee?"

"Hmph." Rosalee paused, tilted her head and crossed her arms. For a woman who had spoken so few words over the past several years, Rosalee's body language strongly suggested a rather surly mood, as she stood before the woman her beloved son trusted so much.

"You say 'this evening' as if I stop by on occasion, when, if I recall correctly, Ms. Martha, I ain't never come to your schoolhouse before today."

Although she didn't know exactly why Rosalee was there, Martha knew the matter between the two of them involved Gabriel and so, even if she had to endure Rosalee's elusiveness, even if Rosalee became outright rude, Martha was determined to give the woman she greatly respected and genuinely pitied her undivided attention. When she next responded to Rosalee, she coated her voice with as much compassion as her heart could muster.

"I understand Rosalee. So, please, allow me to ask again. What brings you here? Why did you come to see me?"

"Ms. Martha, if we are going to talk, I mean really talk, then I need to know now before I even begin to have my say, I need to know that you gone tell the truth, no matter what it is, no matter how bad. 'Cause I give you my word that this here talk is just between me and you. And you ain't got no reason to not trust me. For years, I done trusted you with my boy, even though I had good reason not to. Still, I did."

Martha could feel her stomach curling with nervousness. Rosalee's tone left nothing to imagine and she accepted their visit was not going to be comfortable. The truth she spoke of was not accompanied by comfort or ease and so she braced herself and gave Rosalee her word.

"Yes. I promise I will tell you whatever you have come here to discover, Rosalee. Although I don't understand why you feel like you shouldn't trust me. I have always given you and your family my utmost respect and I always will. I know it has been strange to y'all for me to be so closely associated with Gabriel, but I promise, I swear to you. I would never do anything to hurt him or place him in harm's way. I assure you. You can trust me, just as I trust you. You can trust me, Rosalee." Martha reiterated.

Rosalee dropped her arms and relaxed her shoulders a bit, as she straightened her back and lifted her chin. She would not beat around the bush. She did not have the time or the energy to small-talk her way to the point of her visit.

"Then….I need you to tell me the truth." As she spoke, Rosalee's stature softened and her shoulders slumped again, denoting the sadness that accompanied her indignation. "You think I done failed him? As a mother, I mean. I have failed my son. Ain't that what you think of me Ms. Martha? I mean, you know just how much I ain't been there for him. Every since, well, every since…."

Martha's sincerity was crystal clear as she interrupted before Rosalee could reference the tragic event that lie at the heart of the matter between them.

"What I know, Rosalee, is how remarkable of a person, a woman, and, yes, a mother, you are to even be able to carry on after such a thing. So, no. I do not think you have failed Gabriel in any way, whatsoever."

"Well, I do. Matter of fact, I know I have. I done failed him day after day, everyday, just about every moment, seems like, since Benjamin was taken away from me. I lost my boy and so I lost my way and gave up. Failed my husband and anybody that ever counted on me before then. But I especially failed Gabriel. I just flat out stopped being there for the child. Just let you take my place with loving and nurturing and caring for him the way I should've been doing. I didn't like you doing it, didn't like him getting it from you and then at the same time I was glad of it, 'cause at least I knew he was getting from somebody. Failing Gabriel done just about broke my heart as much as losing Benjamin did. Nothing I can do about Benjamin. But I am hoping by coming here today, I can do better by Gabriel."

"How can I help you, Rosalee?" Martha all but pleaded.

"By telling the truth. You want me to trust you? You want to help me? Well, the only way you can help me is by helping Gabriel. And seems to me that the only way for you to really help Gabriel is by you telling the truth."

Martha slightly shook her head in wonder before replying to Rosalee's vague demand.

"I don't know what you mean. I have helped Gabriel. For years now, I've hardly done anything else but help Gabriel and the other children on this farm. It's the only reason why I am here. I live right here, as close to the Quarters as one can get just so I can help."

Rosalee spoke slowly and deliberately.

"Now see. That is why I don't trust you. You don't tell the truth."

Martha arose from her desk, walked over to the bench by which Rosalee was standing and sat down. Somewhat dazed and confused by the confrontational tone in Rosalee's voice and shaking her head in protest of the accusation against her of dishonesty, Martha began to resign herself to the reality of the purpose of Rosalee's visit. The very thought of what Gabriel's mother wanted her to do caused Martha to begin to tremble. Her anxiety did not escape Rosalee, who knew she had to capitalize on Martha's nervousness and vulnerability in order to restore her role not only as Gabriel's mother but also as his caretaker. Rather than soften her approach and allow Martha some time to regain her composure, Rosalee decided to lay it all on the line, in spite of the impact her doing stood to have on her son's devoted teacher and regardless of the potential danger for them all. Gabriel's entire life and future were at stake and so Rosalee pressed forward.

"You and I both know that the only way things gone work out for Gabriel is if you tell the truth," she said, speaking matter of factly. "Maybe you can't or just won't say the truth to me, but you don't have to. Don't you think maybe it's time that you tell the truth as to why you here, all the way down here living in the Quarters, just about, with us, people you ain't got nothing in common with?"

Rosalee didn't give Martha the time to so much as utter a single word. Without pause, she got right to the point she had come to make. As she continued speaking, she was emphatic.

"I already know and I am sure I ain't the only one to know. Just as I am sure nobody else in the Quarters will so much as breathe a word of it, especially to your face. Just as I am sure that my having the nerve to speak of it just may cost me my life. I can't worry about that, not when my child is suffering the way he is and not when, as you and me both know, there is so much more he will suffer if you don't tell it."

"Tell what? And to who?" Martha asked, although inside her heart she knew exactly what Rosalee meant and why she was so adamant. If told, the truth about who she was and why she had chosen her way of life could change everything about Gabriel's situation.

Rosalee motioned for Martha to make room and as she sat down on the bench, she decided to carry out the rest of their conversation, woman-to-woman, soul-to-soul. She knew the gravity of what she was asking and she knew she had shaken Martha to the core. Indeed, the stakes for them all were high and Martha was not exempt from the possible harm that would surround the Lovemans as a result of any revelation of Martha's secret. When she spoke again, Rosalee's voice was determined but also compassionate.

"You can start by telling yourself the truth," she said, placing her hand gently on Martha's hands, which were tightly folded in her lap. "The truth about who you really are and why you are really here. You say you are here to help us, help our children, help my Gabriel. But I say you are really here to help yourself. All this while, all these years, you done satisfied your ownself soul by living down here away from your birthright, living out here on the edge between your real world and ours, out here where you are safe. Safe from being white and safe from being colored. You even get to sleep good at night, falling off to sleep telling yourself how much you done helped the poor little colored children who ain't got no future except that what is out there in those wretched fields they gone have to work for the rest of their lives with little to nothing to show for it. I am sure you sleep even better when you spend your day or some part of it with my Gabriel. You done convinced yourself that all that extra work, all those hours you done dedicated to him, well that alone shows how much you want to be such a help to us colored people. But you got to know, you must know, that all you really doing is helping yourself. Surely, you know that."

At that point, Martha became defiant as she listened to Rosalee basically call her a hypocrite. Had she not given up her entire life for the sake of the school and teaching the children of the Quarters? Had she not given up on her very own one and only true love to stay behind at a place she could never truly consider to be her home? For the sake of helping others, was she not very much homely and lonely, without a family of her own, with no husband and no children? By helping them, had she not denied herself so very much?

As if she had read every single one of the thoughts racing through Martha's mind, Rosalee continued.

"Oh, I know you think you have helped. I am sure you believe that the good you have done- and yes, indeed, Ms. Martha, you have done plenty good for many folks around here, especially my Gabriel- I am sure you believe that done so for the sake others besides yourself. But I am here today to declare that the good you done so far has been more for you than for anybody else, including Gabriel. Living here and teaching these children is how you done set yourself aside. It is how you have separated yourself and lived beyond the ways of other white folks. In a strange way you and me, well, we are alike when it comes to being able to pull ourselves away from our real life and that way we don't have to deal with the hand God gave us. Just like I know I got to get back to living, really living in my world, even though that world got hardly anything but grief for me, I think you know that if you are really going to help us, you got to do so from inside your world, not out here outside of it. And if you are really going to help Gabriel at all, you got to start by declaring yourself as who you really are and telling the truth. You got to tell the truth, Ms. Martha, at least to yourself and then to the one other person who can make the difference here that we most certainly need made."

The sound of Rosalee breathing deeply caused Martha to lift her head. They had not made eye contact while sitting together on the bench. Seeing the tears streaming down Rosalee's cheeks caused her own eyes to water. In a voice heavily laden with a mother's love, Rosalee spoke again, almost in a whisper.

"I know what I am asking of you. And I know what can happen if things go wrong. I know if you do what I am asking you are putting your own life at risk and, still, I am asking you to do it. If you do what I am asking, what I am begging you to please, please do, there is at least a chance that Gabriel will be alright. More than alright, he may just get to be the man he is supposed to be, the man he was born to be. I know you love him. I know you believe in him. But you haven't really helped him, not yet, not until you put it all on the line for him."

As she stood to prepare to leave, Rosalee's parting words pierced Martha to the core.

"You see, Ms. Martha. All that you have done for us here in the Quarters and everything you have given up in order to do so has been your choice. You could have gone the other way, lived some great life, maybe been the very pearl of your society. But you chose instead to come and live with us and to teach our children. Your choices may not have brought you a rich husband and pretty lily white children, a mansion, fine clothes and all the things white people get at the hands of those of us who have no choices to make. Everything has already been decided for us. Where we live, who we marry, what time we awake, what we eat and how long we sleep. And now, here we have one who maybe, just maybe, will truly get to see life for what it is and how God intended it to be even with his having the skin color he has. My heart is beating simply for that chance, the chance that Gabriel will get to make his own choices for his life. But that is up to you. You say you want the best for him. You say you love him and that teaching him has done you good. Let you tell it, you never, ever knew anybody, white or colored, as special as Gabriel. Ain't that what you say to just about anybody who will listen? You see, your choices brought you Gabriel, if nothing else. So you ended up with the finest life has to offer after all and I know, yes, I know, you really do love him. What I do not know is if you will act like you do."

And without awaiting a response, Rosalee stood up, turned her back and walked out the door.

Chapter Nine

MAIDENS AND MENDACITY

For most people, the transition from childhood to adulthood is a blurred memory and at best, most folks can think back to a period, a general time frame of a couple years when childish ways and thoughts lessened and grown-up ideas and endeavors began to dominate their mindsets and personalities. Martha envied those folks. She had long wished that she had lived the luxury of a typical coming of age, but such had not been her fate. She knew exactly when she had gone from girl to woman. She remembered vividly the day when her childhood ceased to exist and her innocence was lost. She did not make the transition alone. Three children became adults that day, three children who had all spent their wonder years together as playmates, frolicking in the fields of the Peterson Plantation, laughing their way through games and antics, sharing secrets of hideaway places and discoveries that serve as a delight to the young at heart. For eleven years, they had been inseparable, their status as children affording them the luxury of interaction despite their differences. Unlike the clear and distinct separation of the races and the sexes that was the societal norm of the South, children, at least for the first few years, were exempt. Boys and girls played alongside one another with equal rank and white children and black children maintained relationships that were governed by their imagination and not the ills of racism and white supremacy. Usually the exemption only applied to the first five, maybe six years of the lives of those born on the Peterson Plantation. Because the bond between the Peterson twins and their wet nurse's daughter was so obvious and so natural, their childhood ties had been granted an extension past the time gender and race became the determining factor for the formation of relationships, before racial lines were drawn and white children took on the ways of their parents and started to put their former playmates of color in their "place" by treating them more like property than peers.

The day Martha transformed from a little girl to a young woman was deeply embedded in her memory. That day changed her world from a place filled with joy and oblivion to the realities of her southern situation into a legion of sadness, regret and remorse—a new world that demanded her keen awareness of being born into an era and living in a place where hatred and ignorance were the drivers of decisions of those empowered by the senseless fortune of being born into the white race. Suddenly, Martha had been alerted to her existence as a white woman living in a time when love and compassion were merely indicators of weakness and frailty, if and whenever spoken or demonstrated toward people of color. In Martha's real world, white people did not belittle themselves or their race by having regard for the well-being of those who were born only for the purpose of rendering service and accomplishing the work that was the best suited for those they deemed to be a lesser people. The day that Martha became a woman was the same day she discovered the stark incompatibility between her natural self and her social surroundings. That day triggered her station in life as a misfit and sparked her quiet rebellion against the wicked reality of southern tradition. The years since her youthful days and all the lies and the truths that dwelled within them had equipped her with a determined pride and a strong sense of self-assurance. With good reason, that day so long ago stood out in her mind as the defining moment of her life. Second only to the lynching of Benjamin Loveman, the horror that happened that day—the day she would never be able to forget, was the most heinous, the most deplorable and despicable of acts. Of all the terrible instances of violence against the colored people of the Peterson Plantation, this attack was the one that she carried in her heart and the one that lingered in Martha's mind many days of her lonely life. Time had refused to erase that dreadful day. How and why everything happened were recurring thoughts that Martha could never escape, mostly because of who was attacked and just as much because of the identity of the culprit and why he did what he did that day so long ago.

Martha Scott Peterson was born a twin. Although her twin was a boy and though they physically had very little in common, cosmically, they were connected in the emotional way that is unique to twin siblings. They were both happy, free-spirited children, who could spend hours on end together and never tire of one another's company. Martha and her twin brother were so close, there was so much love and trust between the two of them, so much chemistry and synergy of character, that they hardly had any need for the company of other children, that is, with the exception of Hannah. When you saw the Peterson twins, you saw Hannah James. She matched them in age and size and childish glee and she had been at their side from day one, when her mother, who had birth her just a few weeks before, was tasked as the nurse maid for the precious newborn Peterson twins. Hannah's mother had cared for Martha and Robert, doted on them as if they were her very own and was much more nurturing toward them than their own biological parents. As her mother raised the twins from plump, freckle-faced babies to mischievous toddlers to idealistic and curious youngsters, little Hannah had benefited from their closeness with their wet nurse and caretaker, for the Petersons had looked the other way when it came to Hannah's constant presence in their home. For the first eleven years of her life, she ate, played and slept with Martha and her twin brother, as if she was a member of the Peterson family. Martha loved her dear friend as much as any girl could love a sister and the two of them runnings through the fields hands held tightly or huddling together in the underbrush sharing girlish secrets was a common sight. Just as common and frequent was the scenery of Hannah wading in a creek or climbing a tree with Martha's twin brother, Robert, at her side or on her heels. For years, everyone, white and colored, looked upon the relationship between Hannah and the Peterson twins as the innocent and pure luxury of childhood, a time when gender and race were not nearly as meaningful as the shared interests of fun and laughter. Everyone, including their parents, Richard and Wilma Peterson, took the closeness of Hannah, her twin brother and their darling playmate in stride and everyone accepted the simple fact that they doted on their beloved Hannah, and considered her their equal, everyone, that is, except Richard, Jr., Martha and Robert's older brother, who, perhaps, was the meanest Peterson ever born.

Richard Peterson, Jr. had always despised his twin siblings' relationship with Hannah, who he never called by her name but always referred to as "that nigga girl". He especially loathed his little brother's obvious affection for the little "pickaninny" and considered Robert's friendship with her an embarrassing display of weakness and a blemish up the reputation of a family long held as one of the most prominent and avid subscribers of the ideology of white supremacy. For years, Richard Jr. had tolerated his younger brother's relationship with the skinny, little daughter of their nanny, but as they all approached the age of twelve, Richard Jr. decided the time had come for his twin siblings, especially his brother, to learn the facts of life and to draw the line between them and the nigger they loved so much. Martha Peterson remembered the day Richard Jr. made his decision, remembered that day vividly, for that was the last day of her naivety, the day her twin brother, Robert, became a rapist and a distinguished young man of the South. Hannah had narrowly escaped death that day. After enduring a beating and the brutal raping of her virginity by the friend she had come to love so much, she had pleaded with him not to kill her. Her cries, her pleas had competed vigorously with his brother's demand that Robert "finish her off." Miraculously, after raping Hannah, Robert had been immediately consumed with a sense of guilt that momentarily outweighed his dire desire to please his older brother. When he gave Hannah a few seconds to collect herself and run off into the woods he had simultaneously closed the door to his brother's affection and approval, forever.

∞

Most years, the close of summer on the Peterson Plantation was signified by a series of daily rainstorms, that were often relentless with wind shear and flash floods. Without fail, at least one or two storms during this phase of the planting season would be so violent, so hazardous, work in the fields would be brought to a halt. After several laborers had been struck dead by lightning while working amongst their families and neighbors, Robert Peterson had learned the hard way to gage the weather and relieve his laborers from exposure to the most dangerous of storms, rather than run the risk of losing another source of labor and income. Reluctantly, he would instruct his field manager to "let the niggers come in from the rain." The time away from the fields was a rare treat for those who worked pretty much from sunup to sundown, day in and day out and few things excited folks in the Quarters more than a sudden blackened sky in the middle of the day or a booming clap of thunder early in the morning.

Thunder had rolled loudly on the same morning that Ella's conscience had awakened with enough courage for her to deal with the matters of her own heart. The very occurrence of such a storm was indicative of how the time was fast approaching for Gabriel to make a decision and she needed to find a way to sort through the conflicting thoughts whirling through her mind. They were as torrential as the morning's rainfall and both Ella's thoughts and the rain overwhelmed her as she made her way to the schoolhouse to see Ms. Martha. She needed to talk to somebody right away and her mother would not do. There was no way she could share her dilemma with Rosalee, for doing so was certain to break Gabriel's confidence and possibly bring the shame of his mother's disapproval upon her. Her teacher, Ms. Martha, was the only person she could trust and, somehow, Ella felt that the woman was not likely to pass harsh judgment on her for what she was contemplating. Even if she did, though, the risk had to be taken, for the longer Ella kept her thoughts to herself the more tempted she was to act on them, though her doing so could ruin things for Gabriel and for herself, as well.

For weeks Ella had been in despair, going back in forth in her mind as to whether or not she should give Gabriel her virginity. Had the letter never come, she would have never even had to consider the matter, for in her heart, there was only one man for her. Being with him in an entirely intimate way would have happened without hesitation or reservation. She and Gabriel would be like any other young couple in the Quarters who got together and stayed with their families until Robert Peterson saw fit to assign them their own cabin, an assignment that usually came along the same time as a baby or two. Like everyone else they knew, they would have their babies, live in that cabin, work those fields and go about their very hard lives with barely anything more than their love for each other and their families to bring them joy. Now that the letter had come, they would never be like the other young lovers of the Quarters and Ella found herself driven to Gabriel by more than just her desire for him. Every since he had told her about the letter, the decision Gabriel had to make had ignited Ella's passion and she found herself tempted to offer her body to Gabriel for more than one reason. The best of her imagination was convinced that she should give herself to him because, if he decided to go, she may not ever have the chance to become his wife and the mother of his children, though she had always dreamed such was to be her fate. Although some would think she was wrong and a certain sinner for doing so, Ella wanted to give herself to Gabriel completely, even if for only one encounter. If she couldn't be with him forever, she wanted and needed the memory of the two of them together, a memory she was certain to cherish for the rest of her life.

As much as she wished a precious memory was her only motivation for making love to Gabriel, deep in the back of Ella's thoughts was the hope that fate would overtake their lovemaking and that before he could leave, they would discover they had made more than love. In her heart, in the same place where her fears resided, Ella secretly hoped that if she gave Gabriel her virginity, she would become pregnant with his child. As far as she was concerned, theirs was the kind of love destined to make a baby the first time their bodies became one. Indeed, if she became pregnant with his child, that circumstance would provide Gabriel the perfect excuse to forego the offerings of the acceptance letter, for surely he would not compromise her honor or their love for one another by going so far away. If Gabriel knew she was carrying his child, he would remain at Peterson Plantation to take care of her, their child and the rest of his family. Ella had even convinced herself that perhaps their child would be the one destined to act upon the genius that was sure to be passed on to him or her from Gabriel. Whenever Ella allowed herself to acknowledge what she was thinking and actually hoping, she became riddled with guilt and shame. That she could ever consider manipulating Gabriel in such a way made her feel unworthy of his love and ashamed of her own, for her adoration was driving her to foolish thoughts. Though her temptation was not as strong as her hope for Gabriel's best life, the notion still lingered and she found herself afraid of her own will. There was only one person she trusted with her secret thoughts. Somehow, Ella knew that if she found the courage to say what she was thinking aloud, she was far less likely to act on her temptation.

∞

That morning's rainstorm had kept everyone out of the fields and the school children home for some rare quality time with their parents. School being dismissed for the day gave Ella just the time and chance she needed to visit with Ms. Martha alone. Her mentor was sitting reading quietly when Ella entered the classroom. Hearing the bustle of wet footsteps across the ragged wooden floor, Martha lifted her head to see her most precious student approaching. Ella walked into the schoolhouse with her head hanging and shoulders sagging but, still, there was a maturity about her carriage and, in that moment, Martha noticed how much of a woman her favorite girl had become over the course of the summer. Though tiny and frail in form, Ella was stunningly beautiful and, over the years, she had blossomed into the sweetest, kindest of souls. Martha's love for her was genuine and deeply rooted.

When Martha looked up and saw Ella standing right in front of her, a shiver ran through her entire body, for the young maiden was almost an exact replica of the woman who was the tie between the two of them. Ella's lighter skin tone was the only physical difference between the two women. In all else, in stature, posture, frame and features, Ella was her mother's duplicate. Seeing her standing there with such a tortured expression upon her face, hastened Martha's thoughts back to the day that her long lost childhood friend, Hannah, had returned to the Peterson Plantation.

Years before, it had been Ella's mother, Hanna, who had appeared solemnly in the schoolhouse doorway. Although she was shocked to see her childhood friend, she was also extremely relieved that the friend lost to her so long ago had come back to her. Time had taken a toll, though, and Hanna's thin, fragile body bore the stress of their years apart. The cruelty and sadness of her life was featured in Hanna's face, which, though still beautiful, was sagging with weary and grief. Still, despite the show of time and pain, Martha had instantly recognized Hanna. They had known each other all of their lives and though unspeakable circumstances had kept them at a distance for more than six years, they had never forgotten their childhood bond or the day they had been driven apart. The matter that brought her back was urgent and Hanna's situation did not allow her any time to spare for reintroductions and nostalgic greetings. She had come back to Peterson Plantation because Martha was the only person who could possibly, would possibly, help her and her little girl, Ella. Each and every passing moment weighed against Hannah and even more against her only child and so in a hushed but very deliberate voice she stated her reason for being there.

"My husband done died, Ms. Martha." She really did not have to explain anything else beyond the announcement of her husband's death. Both women were fully aware of the implications of Hanna's loss. Yet, Hanna had shown up that day to make the urgency of her matter plain and clear to the one person in the world who just might give a damn about the welfare of Hannah and her daughter. Looking Martha squarely in the eyes, she continued.

"Won't belong before menfolk, white and colored come after her. One of my neighbors didn't even wait 'til my poor husband was cold with death before he tried. Had to fend him off with my axe." Martha's eyes asked the unspeakable question which was met with Hanna's reassurance that the assault was a failed attempt and also a stark indicator of just how much danger surrounded Hannah and her child now that the woman had no husband to protect them.

"I got him away that time. But I'm weak and I'm getting weaker by the day. That child been the only reason I even tried to be strong thus far. Was not for her, I'd be more than satisfied to be in the dirt right alongside my husband."

Hannah paused before continuing, knowing full well that what she next would say would be a heavy push against an emotional door that she and Martha both had avoided opening for the past few years. Due to her husband's sudden death of a heart attack in the field a week and a half earlier, Hannah had no other choice. Except for her dearly devoted husband and the poised and kind-natured woman who was once like a sister, only one other person would understand why she had ventured onto the Peterson Plantation in search of shelter and protection for her and her daughter. Hannah knew better than to ever go to that person in her distress. She knew that her only possible chance rests within the heart and mind of the woman standing before her, the one who was listening as if her own life was at stake, the one who had yet to say a word, but was nodding anxiously for Hanna to keep explaining her plight.

*As if saying what she needed to say softly and swiftly would somehow main-
tain the secret the two women shared, when she spoke again, Hanna had lowered
her voice even more and rushed the next words out of her mouth.*

"She don't know nothing. Except she look funny. She think it some kind of
fluke of nature that she so light with white folk hair. She don't know. Nobody
know how except you and him and my dead husband and he took that secret to
the grave right along with his love and his care for her and me. Ain't nobody to
look after her now and I'm so scared that the same thing that happened to me is
gone happen to her."

*If indeed Hanna's fear, nightmare rather, ever materialized Martha knew
she would be riddled with a guilt that she would not be able to endure. For years,
she had tried to shake the memory of the terrible act that almost killed Hannah.
What bothered Martha most was not only what happened but how it had all
come to happen so suddenly and how helpless she had felt when she had failed to
understand how much danger Hannah was set to encounter in the hands of her
brothers. She herself been shocked and depressed for years over the savage rape
and beating that Hannah had barely survived, her shock and unrest rooted not
only in the fact the hideous act had occurred but also in the tortuous reality of
who had committed such an awful transgression against the girl she had known
since they were both babes. Still, Martha's melancholy paled in comparison to her
guilt, guilt that she wasn't there to stop the attack, guilt that as much as she and
Hanna actually had in common, she was not likely to ever be at risk of such a
violence happening to her simply because she was white and wealthy. More than
anything, Martha was burdened with the guilt of being so naive to the harsh realities of living and loving in Chester County and being an heir to the Peterson legacy.*

*The guilt she had lived with for years plagued Martha and kept her from truly
seeking her own personal happiness. That same guilt also drove her to commit
her time, her energy and her own personal finances to educating the children of
Peterson Plantation. She was more than a teacher. She was a counselor, a confidant and a friend to the children she taught, who all trusted her to do her best to
educate and protect them. As she stood there that day, hearing and receiving the
plea of her long lost childhood friend, she had vowed to herself that she would
protect Hannah's daughter with every fiber of her being. Martha had compassion*

for all the folks who lived on the Peterson Plantation, but she had always dearly loved Hannah, even all the while they were separated, and she had always loved Hannah's child, a child she had never seen but had known about for years. Hearing Hanna's prediction of the harm that was destined to come the child's way unless she took the matter under her control was heartbreaking and when she responded, the dogged determination in Martha's voice was as clear as a bell.

"It won't." she said defiantly. "I won't let that happen to her. I give you my word. I'll look after her, Hanna. I'll look after her every day the good Lord sees fit to give me breath and as long as I'm living, no harm will come her way. Anybody that wishes to do anything to her, anything at all, will have to kill me first. Nobody is going to hurt that child and nobody is going to hurt you ever again. I know you only came to me because you had nowhere else to go. I know you probably didn't want to on account of who I am and how close we are were way back then. I know you think I failed you. And if you don't then you should know that I think I did and I feel it every day. I don't know if you hate me or not. I hope and pray you don't because I would give anything to go back to that day. But if you do hate me, your love for your child is stronger than that hate and for that I'm grateful. You've been through so much and I know you're scared to come here. But I swear to you right here and right now that you and that child will be safe here. I will see to everything. You just get ready to go back right away, now. I'll get someone from the Quarters to take you back so you can collect your things. You get everything and come right back. Move you and the girl in with your sister and explain nothing to nobody. If anybody has questions-"

Martha paused and then shook her head as she spoke again.

"They won't. But, if they do, tell them to come and see me. Your sister's cabin is big enough and it will do both of you some good to be together. Work in fields, Hanna only if you can and just to keep talk down, but, again, only if your health allows it and you want to. Otherwise, you can just say you do daily work around my house for me. Of course, I don't want you to lift a finger. If you ever do, I will be most offended. This is not pity. This is friendship. As for Ella, send her to me -everyday. She'll go to school and when she gets to the age when she's expected to work, well, she'll work for me by going to school some more."

131

As she concluded, her voice had begun to tremble ever so slightly and she made her final statement with her eyes closed, for fear her dear old friend would see right through her and right into the core of her guilt over all that had happened. One tear slid down Martha's cheek as she lowered her head and said, "She simply cannot work in the fields. I will not see her there."

The next day, only a few days after her sweet, dear daddy had died, Ella and her mother moved into her Aunt Alberta's cabin on the edge of the quarters of the Peterson Plantation and only a few plots of land over from Ms. Martha's schoolhouse. Now here it was some twelve years and in the same doorway of the same school Ella herself had appeared.

Noticing her standing there as if she brought the world's weight along with her, Martha couldn't help but to gaze in awe of Ella's beauty. The years had subtly changed her from the solemn-faced, shy but strikingly beautiful little girl to the quiet but obviously assertive young woman who was physically gorgeous and, better yet, remarkably sweet and considerate in spirit. Though hardly a day passed when she didn't see Ella, somehow, on that particular day, the distance between her desk and the doorway was far enough for Ella's entire person to be seen, yet close enough for Martha to take in every detail of the young lady she had come to cherish so very much.

At a closer glance, Martha could not help but notice the worrisome expression spread across Ella's lovely face and she found herself standing and reaching out for an embrace. As the girl she loved as her very own caved into her arms, Martha could sense her sadness. Indeed, Ella was both sad and anxious and without Martha's prompting, the young woman poured out her feelings and fears, speaking so rapidly Martha immediately understood the urgency of her matter and the depth of her despair. Seeing Ella looking so afraid and caring so deeply for the man she loved, Martha became overwhelmed with her own emotions. Instantly, she thought of the charge she had received from Rosalee just a few days before and, taking one look at Ella, who seemed to be in need of her help, Martha knew in her heart the time had come for her to begin her journey toward the truth. Lifting Ella's face by her chin so that she and her protegee' could stand eye to eye, Martha began to speak.

"Have you ever wondered why I was so dedicated to Gabriel all these years? Why I understand the way he thinks so much?" she asked.

Through her sniffles, Ella responded. "Because....because y'all are so much like each other."

"Well, no, now that's why I'm so dedicated to you, my dear. You and I are so very much alike. You see, we both know what it is like to love a man who is destined for greatness and the heartbreak that comes along with that love."

She could see that Ella was bewildered by her confession. Martha had never spoken about her one and only true love. For years, she had managed to tuck the memory of him far back in a tiny crevice of her heart and seldom ever did she allow herself to revisit their love and heartbreak. Ella's anguish and her apparent struggle with the idea of a separation from Gabriel was so familiar that Martha knew she had no choice but to share her story with Ella. The young woman standing alongside her reminded her so very much of herself for so many reasons, but especially because of the love she so obviously felt for the other person to whom Martha was so deeply connected. Ella was deserving of her truth, her sacred truth. Telling her the truth was the only way Martha could really help her, or so it seemed. She drew in a deep breath and began to speak again.

"Ella, dear, sweet Ella, I want you to know that I understand exactly how you feel. You see, my friendship with Gabriel is not the first time I have had the joy of knowing someone extra special. When I was your age I loved someone. I loved him the way you love Gabriel. He was a splendid boy and I adored him. He was from the next county over and our families were longtime acquaintances and friends. I didn't know him all that well when we were youngsters but when we reached the proper age for such, I began to see him at all the social gatherings for young ladies and men. Right away I noticed he was different from my brothers and all the other young men I knew. I am sure most folks around here considered him odd, but his family was wealthy and so even if they thought he was strange, hardly anyone was going to say so. I knew he wasn't strange, though. It only took me a couple of conversations to know why he stood out from all the rest, why he didn't seem to fit in with all the other boys from around these parts and what I discovered about him made my heart skip, stole my breath away, yes it did."

As she continued, she could sense Ella's shifting from a state of anxiety to a more curious mood. Still, they held onto each other and maintained their gaze into each other's eyes. The moment had become one of the sweetest of Martha's lives and with each word, she found the truth rising up from the secret cavities in her heart and flowing across her lips. As much as Ella needed to hear her life story, Martha needed to share and the love she once felt was deserving of her openness with the one she had watched grow from girl to woman. As she spoke, Martha began to smile and her voice softened, as the memories of her young love flooded through her mind.

"You see, he was a good person, the kind of person who wanted nothing to do with a way of life that involves the mistreatment of others for the sake of one's own personal gain. I don't know how he got to be that way. It seems impossible since, white boys are told from day one that they are superior and entitled, that the manner in which they treat their wives and children, their employees and especially colored people is justified, for such is necessary for the establishment of their manhood and the increase of their wealth. He never believed it though. He could never make sense of hurting and abusing other people in order to make his own way through life. I felt like I met my own very self, only in the form of a boy. We became fast friends. We told each other everything, shared all of our dreams and secrets and, soon enough, we were in love."

" You were in love, Ms. Martha?' Ella exclaimed in almost disbelief.

" Indeed I was. And very much so. He was handsome and he was kind. And, my goodness, he was incredibly smart. Not as smart as

Gabriel, I must admit, but not too far behind him. The difference between him and Gabriel, though, is that when the time came for him to decide the best course for his life, he did not have to worry about what that decision would mean for his family. His father was disappointed that he did not want to live in the South, but he loved him and when he told his parents he wanted to go to the East Coast for college, they sent him off in grand style, with all of his expenses for his education paid well in advance. They made sure he had a fine place to live and even arranged for him to have a staff to take care of his personal needs. And they even went as far to speak with my parents to assure them that my acceptance of his proposal would also include their support of me."

" You were ENGAGED?"

Martha paused and drew another deep breath before responding to Ella's bewilderment.

"No," she said softly, almost whispering. "No. I wasn't. I did not accept his proposal. I couldn't. My place was here. I could not leave Peterson Plantation, although in my heart, I wanted desperately to marry him, to be with him."

A sudden rush of sadness overcame Martha as she recalled how devastated both she and her young beau had been when she rejected his offer of marriage. She made no effort to contain herself, for she wanted Ella to know how very much she understood why she had come to her that day. She wanted Ella to know just how safe a space she would always create for her and why.

"When I told him that my life's calling was to set up the school and to watch over the children who would come through it, we cried. He even contemplated staying behind and going to the State University. But I couldn't let him do that. I knew that just as much as I belonged here, that he did not. So we promised to always love each other and he made me swear that if I ever changed my mind or if I ever needed anything, I would contact him right away. I didn't even attend his going away party. While everybody was sending him off, I busied myself by working on this schoolhouse and getting it ready for my first school term."

Martha slightly chuckled and shook her head, as she relayed her heartbreak to Ella.

"I cried so much we almost didn't even need to stain the floors, but in a few days, he was gone and I was teaching my first class."

" You never saw him again?" Ella asked, her voice quivering with alarm and pity.

" Once." Martha replied, matter of factly. "He came home for his daddy's funeral a few years later. He had the prettiest wife and a precious baby boy with him and I remember that I was relieved that he was happy."

"I don't think I could be glad to see Gabriel with someone else." Ella said, her voice filled with defiance.

Martha understood exactly what she meant and how she felt. Chuckling again, she clarified herself.

"Oh, I didn't say all of that, Ella. I knew I would always love him, but I also accepted that it wasn't to be if we both were to be true to ourselves. I was just glad that at least one of us also obtained the fulfillment that comes from having a family."

"And so Gabriel reminds you of him and you think me and you are the same?" Ella asked, as she stood up straight and pulled away from Martha. "You trying to tell me to let him go, huh, Ms. Martha? That's why you telling me this here sad love story of yours?"

Martha knew that what she was saying was difficult for Ella to hear. She also knew that they would not be having the conversation if Ella didn't trust her to tell the truth.

"I am telling you that I understand how much you love him and that yes, that I do believe you will let him go."

"How can you be so sure I will be as strong as you?" Ella asked, as thoughts of her recent temptations consumed her mind.

"Because, Ella, my dear, as I said a few minutes ago, you and I are more alike than you know."

With that Martha took Ella back into her arms and held her as tight as she could. The young woman cried softly, at first, and then wept uncontrollably as she reconciled her heart with her determined mind. She would not stand in Gabriel's way and she would not ever again consider doing or saying anything that suggested she did not support a decision on his part to leave, even if that meant the two of them would be separated for good. Once she collected herself, she sat up and looked her mentor straight in the eyes. They had shared a very heavy and personal moment and she felt closer to her teacher than ever.

"Thank you. I don't know how I can show it, but I thank you so much."

"Thank me by cleaning that gosh awful chalkboard and setting up this classroom for tomorrow." Martha said with another chuckle, hugging Ella again, this time briskly and reassuringly.

Just as Ella stood to begin her tasks, Martha reached up and pulled her back down. She figured, given what she was about to say, they both would fare better if they were sitting still.

"Ella, I need to tell you something. I think that if I don't tell you now I may never get enough courage to tell you and you deserve to know.

Ella's heart immediately sank with a gut-wrenching pain. "He's already decided to go, hasn't he? That's why you told me what you told me. You are trying to prepare me."

"No, no, no.....no! It's not that. I don't know that just yet. He hasn't told me either. Besides there are just so many things. Mr. Robert, the money, his family's health, the whole Benjamin situation and you. Ella, he loves you just as much you love him. So, no, I want him to go. You right about that but I do not know if he will and I am doing all I can to let that be his decision."

"So what do you have to tell me? What is it? Is it bad, Ms. Martha? You look like it is bad."

Martha placed her hand on the anxious girl's shoulders in an attempt to brace her for the shock of what she was about to hear.

"Sit still, Ella. Just sit still now. I need you to just let me say this while I have the nerve."

With that, Martha, drew a deep breath and released the secret that had been tormenting her for years. Hearing what Martha had kept hidden for so many years would have knocked Ella over if she hadn't already been sitting down. Her knee jerk reaction was to move away as quickly as she could, but Martha had anticipated her alarm and had tightened her grip on Ella's arms, holding her steady in place.

"Listen to me. Don't move. Don't say a word. Just listen to me, please child. Will you do that? Just sit here and listen to me explain?"

Ella nodded, as tears began to flow down her cheeks, tears of confusion and wonder. Still, she could see the compassion, the hope in Martha's eyes and she knew to trust the woman who had always been kind and loving to her. And so she listened as her teacher, her mentor, her aunt recalled how her mother had experienced the tragic horror of being raped and almost killed by her own childhood friend, how Martha had naively watched as Hanna had willingly gone off for a hike with Robert and their older brother that day, and how she had been plagued with guilt of not going with her, not protecting her, not envisioning the evil act that lie in store for her best friend, who she loved with all her heart. She told Ella how for some time after the incident, her family thought maybe Hanna had actually died until they heard of a young colored girl showing up on a neighboring plantation and marrying one of the field hands, only to give birth a few months later to an obviously mulatto girl child. Her father and older brother had condemned her twin for his cowardice and failure to finish off the deed of killing Hanna, thus bringing possible shame to the Peterson family, whose blood had, until then, remained purely white. Indeed, the purity of their bloodline was the Peterson's pride and the basis for their elevated status amongst the wealthiest of southern families. Robert Peterson's spawning of a colored child threatened that heightened status and the overall reputation associated with the Peterson name. Old man Peterson hated his youngest son for his weakness, his mother silently scorned him and his elder brother mocked and ridiculed him for his inability to be hateful enough to kill a nigger. Martha was devastated by the entire matter and isolated herself from her family as much as she could. She especially distanced herself from Robert, although doing so ripped her heart into pieces.

Over the years, the rejection by his family had embittered Robert Peterson beyond redemption and by the time the rest of their immediate family died, the relationship between him and Martha had deteriorated beyond repair. Even when their older brother died, they barely spoke and did not seek comfort from one another. Their mother died shortly afterwards and by the time their father passed away, they were as distant as strangers. The Peterson estate had been bequeathed to the twins, jointly and equally and Martha had used her legal status as joint owner of the Peterson Plantation to negotiate the school and to try to keep her evil brother from committing even more deplorable acts than he already had. Still, knowing full well the extent of her twin brother's evilness, Martha walked a tight line and chose her battles with Robert Peterson carefully. Sharing this secret with Ella could jeopardize everything, but she could no longer hold it and perhaps now, Ella would understand why she had always kept her close, and why she had always been so protective of her. Her care and devotion wasn't just because the girl was the closest friend to her most brilliant student or because they both were the source of her greatest pride as a teacher. Her efforts weren't only due to Ella being the daughter of her long-lost childhood friend, who had returned to her in need of shelter and help. Her affection was driven by all those things. And even more, it was because Ella was her flesh and blood. Her brother's child and the only family Martha loved. They were both wiping away tears when Gabriel appeared in the doorway.

∞

For the first time in a long time, Gabriel found himself somewhat calm. That day had actually been a good day. The morning thunderstorm had called off work and the late afternoon had gifted them with enough sunlight to enjoy a portion of the evening but not enough to trigger a call to the field. Along with the calmness and the beauty of the day, which had been uneventful and relieving, gracious even, seeing Ella sitting there like a little school girl, eyeing her quiet beauty from the doorway of the school cabin and then noticing her affection for him from the excitement in her eyes when she turned and saw him standing there, had spun up the thought in Gabriel's mind that maybe he was being too dismal whenever he thought of staying. Life wasn't that bad nor was their plight on the Peterson Plantation entirely hopeless. He knew their love would last and there was no doubt that they could marry and have their own family. And in time, perhaps he could even pull them all out of debt. Heck. With time on his side and a little luck, he might even be able to build a proper life for himself, Ella and their families, right there on the Peterson Plantation.

Gabriel didn't know why that day and that particular moment had brought so much to mind. Maybe it was all the extra rest he got that morning when the field manager sent word that there would be no working that day, giving Gabriel the rare treat of being able to sleep late into the morning. Maybe it was the anxiety he felt when he went calling on Ella only to find her gone from her aunt's cabin which was on the opposite side of the Quarters. He had looked for her for more than an hour all over the back fields and around their favorite places to keep private company and had begun to worry until he passed by the school door and caught sight of her long, jet black pigtails and her small frame, as she sat at the front of the classroom with Ms. Martha standing over her. Their posture and demeanor clearly indicated they were in the throes of an intense conversation and when Gabriel cleared his throat, announcing his presence, both women seemed startled and a bit taken aback.

" Ah ha! Y'all up to something...." Gabriel's voice faded as soon as he was close enough to notice Ella's tear stained cheeks. The sad look on her face reignited the worry he had just begun to feel moments earlier when he couldn't find her and he rushed to her side needing immediately to know the cause of her distress.

"What's wrong baby?" he asked, as he gently nudged her shoulder.

Still reeling from the shock of all Ms. Martha had shared and the magnitude of their entire conversation and what it meant for her, her life, and most of all, her love for Gabriel, Ella searched for the right words to avoid lying to him- for she could never bring herself to be dishonest with anyone, especially him. Yet and still, she could not share what she had just been told, not at that moment when Martha's revelation was so fresh and her emotions so raw.

"Oh nothing, really. I was just a bit worried about everything that's been going on and decided to come see Ms. Martha for a little bit. Really, Gabriel, I'm fine." Ella responded, making her best effort to calm Gabriel's concern and to disarm his curiosity. Taking her que from Ella, Martha chimed in quickly, in an attempt to distract him by drawing his attention to his own dilemma.

"I was just telling Ella that I am not aware of your decision or even if you have made one, yet." Martha's tone was a bit more hurried and excited than normal and, right away, Gabriel sensed that he was not being told the entire truth. Somewhat irritated by their secrecy, his reply was curt, as he stood and motioned his head towards the door, indicating to Ella that he was ready for them to leave.

"I haven't made a decision yet. I don't even know if there is a decision for me to make, Ms. Martha. Seems more and more to me, my life is already pretty much established right here at Peterson Plantation."

As he grabbed Ella's hand and walked toward the door, he looked back over his shoulder and smiled. He didn't want to leave his teacher with any bad feelings and he surely didn't want her to think he didn't appreciate all she had done for him. He could see the sadness in her eyes and so he spoke again, just as he and Ella reached the doorway.

"Maybe, if I stay, you and Ella will make room for me sometimes in this schoolhouse. Maybe I can help teach when I am not in the fields. That would be something. I don't know. I mean, if I don't go off to school, that doesn't mean all we have worked for has to go to waste, does it?"

"No, it doesn't Gabriel." Martha replied, with a long sigh. Then, mustering the biggest smile possible, given the gravity of all she was feeling, the teacher nodded toward the two people she loved most in the world, urging them further out the door, as she concluded, "Nothing you have ever done or stand to do, Gabriel Loveman, will ever be a waste."

Martha meant that, meant it more than she could explain. Given the weight of all that already had occurred that afternoon, Martha was relieved they were leaving and she did not want to say anything else that might prolong their departure. She needed time to herself. She needed to think and, after she collected her thoughts, then she needed to act swiftly. Time was of the essence. And so, she bid them goodnight with her usual soft, gracious smile.

"The two of you be careful and enjoy your evening."

As they walked the path way to back to the Quarters, Gabriel decided to do his best to lighten Ella's mood and to take advantage of their very precious time alone.

"Well, I can think of a few things we can do to enjoy our evening." he said, pulling Ella closely into his arms. "As a matter of fact, I've been thinking about a lot of things when it comes to me and you."

"Oh really? And what all might that be?" Ella asked as she nestled her head into the crevice of Gabriel's armpit.

Having his arms around her made her feel safe again and she felt herself calming down from her talk with the teacher and mentor they both loved so much, the woman who was actually her aunt and the brother to the monster who had fathered her when he raped her mother. The thought of all she had just learned caused her to shiver and Gabriel pulled on her tightly.

"You cold, Baby?"

"No, no. I'm fine. You just go on and tell me about all these thoughts."

Gabriel stopped and turned so that the two of them were face to face, while shifting his arms so that he was holding her around her waist. There was still just a hint of light left in the early evening sky and Ella's face seemed to illuminate as Gabriel stared into her big, brown eyes.

"You are so beautiful, Ella." he said softly. "I love you."

Gabriel's declaration had come without warning and Ella suddenly found herself nervous that the two of them were so physically close. She could sense his passion. No one was within ear or eye shot and Gabriel's mood was different. He seemed focused and his focus appeared to be entirely on her. That hardly ever happened. Giving one another their undivided attention was a luxury their life's circumstances hardly ever afforded either one of them. This night was different, though, and Ella could not escape Gabriel's hold on her, not the physical one nor the hold he had on her heart. She realized she had become lost in her own thoughts when he slightly shook her and repeated the question he had just asked after he told her he loved her.

"Will you marry me?"

Stunned and confused, Ella began to cry.

"Now, that is not the answer I was looking for from you, Ella"

Through her soft sobs, she responded.

"You know my answer to that question. There ain't but one answer to that question but what about your schooling, Gabriel? You know I can't leave here. My mama needs me."

"Well, what makes you so sure I am leaving here?" Gabriel chuckled a bit as he wanted to cover his sadness at the thought of giving up his dream. He did not want Ella to ever think or even wonder if being with her was a competing decision, for such was not the case. He just could not see clearly past his shortage of money, the implications for his family if he left and, more than anything, the threat to all of their lives, if Robert Peterson sought the revenge he announced when Gabriel first received his acceptance letter.

Doing his best to reassure the woman who had long been the love of his life, he spoke to Ella, tenderly.

"Look. That mean, old Robert Peterson is not going to live forever. I figure I will stay on here, keep working this land and maybe find some other work that will help get us all out of debt. If nothing else, like I said before we left the schoolhouse, maybe together we can take on the teaching around here. We can raise our children and maybe by the time they grow up, we will have something to pass on to them. I will keep our records so that when all the money is paid, money I am sure has already been paid time and time again, when my record of payment is complete, we can claim our ownership and start our own farm or school or both."

Gabriel was now honestly imagining life with Ella and the thought of their life together and their future children actually excited him. The big smile that had spread across his face as he was relaying his thoughts of their life together faded quickly when he saw Ella's face twisting in horror at his proposition.

Shaking her head, vigorously as she replied, Ella knew she had to take her stance and she knew that, given how much she adored the man holding her so tightly as he detailed their future together, she would not be able to reject him more than once.

"You sound like them old nosey neighbors, the ones always running the young folk down when they decide to leave here. This don't sound like you at all, Gabriel Loveman!" Ella exclaimed. "You the very one always come right back on them old geezers. Ain't you the one who said anybody with a baby's amount of sense ought to know that Robert Peterson rather leave this place to Lucifer himself before he allow us to call the land our own? Now you going along with what the old folks say? No. I don't believe you." she proclaimed, shaking her head in disbelief. "You just trying to lie to yourself and pardon me if I go ahead right now and tell you that you might as well stop it now. You ain't very good at it." Though she stopped speaking, Ella continued to gaze into Gabriel's eyes, as she awaited his response.

There had never been a more intimate moment between them. As much as they had managed to steal away to be alone whenever they could and as much as they had somehow found a way through the years to make countless memories of sweet nothings and inside jokes, Gabriel and Ella had never been as close as they were in this moment. Physically and emotionally they were intertwined in a way that the nature surrounding them seemed to give deference. The clouds above had reconfigured and resituated themselves and so the moon beamed over them, serving as an organic spotlight. The wind shifted and slowed its pace to offer them relief from the heat but without stirring the trees, which stood still, gallant and as green as ever, aligning the pathway as if they were soldiers bearing witness to and protecting the lovers standing under the moonlight clinging to one another for dear life, it seemed.

Something about her indignation intensified Gabriel's yearning for Ella. In that moment, she had transformed completely from girl to woman right before his eyes and, without any doubt, Gabriel knew what he needed to do. Before a second thought could override his decision, he swept off her feet and carried her into the bush, deep into the high soft grass, away from the path and beyond the sight of any passer-bys. Without uttering a word, he took her into his arms and kissed her with a force that caught her so off guard that she almost tripped over her feet. Without interrupting their kiss, he broke her stumble and eased them both to the ground. Ella could not help but be bewildered. She knew that Gabriel loved her and she knew that he was just as much of a man as any but despite their closeness and all the time they spent together, they had always been reserved when it came to physically demonstrating their feelings. In the past, the few times they had acted on their passion for each other had been at her urging. That night something had changed in Gabriel. Something incredibly meaningful was happening. Ella could sense the intensity in the depth and force of his kiss and in the anxious way his hands rubbed her back. For the first time ever, Gabriel pressed his body into hers and she knew what he wanted, what he was about to do. Their intimate embrace continued as day turned into eve and when Ella opened her eyes, she was shocked to see the dark creeping into the sky. She was so aroused, she wanted him so badly she found herself speechless and gasping for her breath. When Gabriel reached his hand under her light cotton dress and slid his warm fingers up her thigh, she lay back without a second's thought, but just as he lifted himself to undo his tattered britches, she caught a faraway look in his eyes and Ella knew that any further movement in the direction they were going would be wrong. Briskly, she sat up and pulled her dress over her knees.

"What's the matter? Isn't this what you want? It's what I want. We both want to do this. We've been wanting to do this."

Gabriel's shaken plea told of his desire for her and on this occasion, unlike any time before, the yearning was immediate. Ella's thoughts scurried for something to say to break their fall from sensibility into the temptation that had been the gravitational pull between them for at least the past two, almost three years. He saw how she was searching for words and before she could speak, he rushed the thought that had been lingering on his mind the whole while he had been kissing her.

"Let's get married tomorrow!" And with that, Ella had pushed Gabriel away from her, jumped to her feet and ran away from him without so much as one word.

Early the next morning, as Gabriel sat alone, praying and preparing his mindset for the upcoming work day, he could not help but ponder the exchange between him and Ella. Hard as he tried, he could not accept any notion that, after all this time and all that they shared, she had really meant to reject him. She knew how much he loved her and that he would never so much as consider being with any other woman or making anyone else his wife. Since most folks who lived in the Quarters did not bother with the makeshift wedding ceremony that Robert Peterson arranged, which pretty much involved everyone gathering up from the fields to take the very few minutes required to watch the marrying jump over a raggedy broom, Gabriel knew Ella's response couldn't have anything to do with her being concerned about them being together before they were "officially" married. Where they lived and how they lived provided a couple with the status of marriage simply by that couple's travel in and throughout the Quarters together, announcing themselves as husband and wife. Many couples would simply wait until the next time everyone could gather for a worship service and while everyone sat around eating and commenting on the sermon or the singing, the newly wed couple would say something to the extent of "Hey everybody! We married." Usually after a couple made such a declaration, one of them would relocate to the cabin where the other lived. Whichever family had the most room typically determined where the couple would first reside together.

Every now and again, there would be talk of some youngsters "running off up North." To give the brave pair's plight an air of romanticism, their kinfolk would announce the fleeing by informing neighbors and friends the young couple had gone North to get married. Most of the time, the couple would never travel beyond the next few neighboring plantations in Chester County. Most often, the so-called newlyweds would be brought back to the Peterson Plantation in the back of a wagon, their bodies lifeless and covered by burlap bags, stinking with the stench of a dual lynching. Such an outcome had occurred so many times that the elderly community within the Quarters had begun to watch young lovers like Gabriel and Ella very closely. Every now and again, when the pair were spotted walking down the path to the fields hand in hand, an older relative or neighbor would approach them and warn, "Don't y'all do nothing crazy. Love is love, no matter where you are, no matter how hard the times, so don't get no crazy notions because y'all is feeling so much love." None of the naysayers had to say specifically what they did not want the couple to do, for the warning went without saying that to try to leave the Peterson Plantation was even more dangerous than living there.

As far as Gabriel and Ella were concerned, though, the elders needn't worry. She had made her intention to always take care of her mother known to Gabriel quite some time ago and they both knew her mother wanted to always be as close as possible to the place where her late husband and Ella's father laid at rest. As far as Gabriel knew, Ella wouldn't leave, wouldn't dare to even think about moving away with him, for doing so would mean leaving her mother behind and, unlike Gabriel, she would not even consider the thought.

Gabriel did not begrudge or resent Ella's resignation. As tempted as he was to leave, the idea of what would become of what was left of his family depressed him more than he had ever imagined. Every time he slightly imagined a life of education and training and working possibly as a professional, actually having a career, Gabriel would become consumed with guilt and a sense of selfishness that he was pretty certain he could not handle on any long-term basis. His family needed him. Benjamin was gone. He was not ever coming back and, without a youthful man to carry the load, the Loveman family, at best, would be at risk of being thrown off the farm and left to ruin. The idea of such, along with his love and devotion to Ella, the woman he knew he would make his wife, burdened his mind that morning and more than ever since he had received the letter of acceptance, his thoughts placed more and more distance between his resolve and the dream he had dreamt since he was old enough to imagine a future. That morning the dream of leaving the South and doing so for the sake of higher learning seemed very much out of reach, no matter what the letter declared.

Never before had Gabriel felt so torn. How do you let go of a dream? Does a dream not serve as the very fuel that moves one through life? To let go of his dream meant that Gabriel would stay on at the Peterson Plantation, that he would live and love as best he could on that miserable farm and that he would die there at the place that bore his brother's death. As he considered his plight, grief filled his heart, yet Gabriel could not bring himself to cry. Besides, as the day began to twinkle through the morning mist, he had no time to do so, anyway, as he could hear his mother calling him in for a bite to eat before the family made their way to field for work. Another day lay before him, another fourteen hours or so of daylight that he would spend in the hot sun, picking, prodding and praying for the coming night and more time for thinking.

Chapter Ten

PITY AND PASSION

F or as long as he had lived with John and Rosalee, David had
always been deferential to his brother and sister-in-law's parental
authority. For several weeks, he had kept quiet and had kept his
thoughts to himself, being fully aware that, for the first time since he
had moved in with his brother's family, he was set to go against the
wishes of John and Rosalee concerning Gabriel. David knew exactly
what his only living nephew should do, what he had no choice but
to do. As hard the decision was for everyone else to make, from
the moment he heard the news that Gabriel had a way to leave the
Peterson Plantation, David considered the resolution to be simple
and undeniable. Gabriel had to go. Anything holding him back from
doing so, no matter how relevant and impactful, was insignificant.
As far as David was concerned, Gabriel had a destiny worth fulfilling.
Everything else, from the family's financial situation, to Gabriel's love
affair with Ella and even the threat against the boy's life and their
lives, meant little in comparison to Gabriel's chance at a better life
far away from the South. In David's opinion, opportunities existed
solely to be taken and though he had remained silent on the matter for
weeks, watching his poor nephew suffer and agonize over the decision before him had just about broken what was left of David's heart.

When he saw Gabriel that day, sitting alone under the tree, looking solemn and conflicted at a time when the boy should have been exuberant and gleeful, David knew the time had come for him to speak up, time for him to say the things his heart had carried for so long.

For days, David had watched his nephew with a close eye. He knew that Gabriel was deeply troubled, but he also knew that there was little chance that the boy would open up to him or to anyone about everything that was bothering him so much for so long. As Gabriel sat alone in his favorite spot under the gigantic oak tree, he looked lonelier than ever and even his posture indicated he felt as if he was carrying the weight of the world over his shoulders, which were hunched over with tiredness and despair. David could tell the boy, the young man, rather, thought he was on his own in his anguish, although nothing was farther from the truth. A conversation between uncle and nephew was long overdue and David decided that evening was as good a time as any for them to have a much needed man-to-man talk.

As he walked down the path to the large oak and stood over Gabriel, the lad did not even lift his head. He had seen his uncle coming and somehow he knew that they were about to embark upon more than a casual "how you doing-what you doing" conversation. After catching a glimpse of his Uncle approaching him, Gabriel braced himself by fixating his eye upon and then deliberately mashing an ant that had been crawling on and around his foot for the last several minutes, as he sat pondering what to do about his life and the choices he needed to make.

"Evening, boy. Looks like you doing more than taking shade under this here old tree." David bellowed, pausing just long enough to see if Gabriel was going to respond. When he didn't, David continued. "Now I don't usually bother you when you steal off to be by yourself. I know you need what little time you get to just rest yourself and that wonderful brain of yours. But something tells me you doing more than resting this evening. Something troubling you, Gabriel?"

As Gabriel sat crouched with his legs tucked under him, his chin resting on his knees, his Uncle David did not belabor the matter before them with more small talk or by waiting for Gabriel to willingly participate in the conversation. Instead, he drew a deep, long breath and began to speak right to the core of Gabriel's conscience.

"Gabriel, I've been watching you boy." he said, emphatically. "Watching you go about your way, day after day, year after year, since Benjamin died. I mean I really been keeping my eye on you, son, and I figure this is the right time for me to tell you something I think you been needing to hear for quite a while now, Gabriel, and that is, simply, you are not your brother. You could never take his place, son, nor are you supposed to. You got no business even trying to do so, even though it's clear to me that's pretty much what you been aiming to do. But you got to live your own life, Gabriel, and, God be my witness, you ought to live it as if Benjamin's death never happened. And then, boy, you have to live your life because his death indeed did happen and because you know better than most people know that this here life the good Lord grants us is not to be trifled with. This life is not at your whim, rather you are at the whim of this life. The only solace you have is that you can make your own choices, your own mark. You can do all you can to make your way through it, as life has its way with you."

David stopped and leaned his back against Gabriel's tree. He needed to choose his next words very carefully. He wanted desperately to encourage Gabriel, but he didn't want to say anything that so shocked or saddened the boy that he hurt him more than he helped him. When he began to speak again, David's voice was calm, steady, and low in volume.

"Some folks say that life happens to us. Other folks believe that we make life happen. I've always thought that the way of life is both of those things combined. You see, Gabriel, in this life, some things are just going to happen to you no matter what you do, no matter what decisions you make. Those things are inevitable and death is one of those things, yes it is. I tell you this, death is as certain as life. As a matter of fact, things are constantly dying all around us. Right now, son, as I speak somebody or something is dying, be it a flower, a bird, a tree or the ant you just stepped on. It could be an old woman, a sick child, a soldier in some war, a beggar on the street or the richest man around. Whoever, whatever, be sure, death is having its way with some soul as I stand here and speak to you under this big old tree. The thing about death, though, is it's got its own selection process and we don't get to weigh in on it. It has no preference, no picks and and no favorites. Death happens to everything and everyone, when time and circumstances so demand and when our heavenly Father so allows. We got no say so in the matter, it seems. And the bigger the life, the bigger the death."

As David paused to catch his breath and carefully align his thoughts so what he wanted to say next would come out with the perfect balance of emphasis and sensitivity, Gabriel finally looked up at his uncle. The day was drawing to a close and dusk was upon them as they lingered under the old oak, but there was just enough light remaining from that day's sun for the two men to clearly see one another's faces. The words his Uncle David spoke had penetrated and pierced Gabriel's heart and though the pain was beyond description, he needed to hear every word David was speaking. Deep down inside, Gabriel already knew the point his uncle was about to make and though he tried to contain himself, the conversation had already moved him and as their eyes met, tears streamed down Gabriel's face.

When David began to speak again, he showed the depth of his compassion for his nephew by placing his hand at the crown of Gabriel's head, slightly urging him to let the tears flow, for they were for his big brother, Benjamin, who they both desperately missed, but who Gabriel had needed especially that trying summer. David had always thought that Gabriel had rushed through the grieving process and except for the initial news of Benjamin's death, he was pretty sure the boy had not shed many tears for his brother. Maybe, out of concern for his parents and probably also out of the comfort that comes with denial, Gabriel, instead, had tucked his grief somewhere deep inside his soul and had refused himself a rightful mourning of the brother he loved so much.

Such was a heavy load for anyone to carry, under any circumstances but given Gabriel's current situation, his uncle was most concerned that if Gabriel did not have a breakthrough, the family was likely to lose him, too, if not to death, to hopelessness. David Loveman was determined to keep that from happening. He knew his nephew well enough to know that while Gabriel had been strong enough to keep his grief out of the sight of his family and others over the past few years, the plight he was facing had compounded the heartache he had long suffered in silence, the kind of heartache that either bitters and stifles a person or, even worse, kills a human being, if not physically, at least emotionally. And so, David was glad to see the tears on his nephew's face, happy for the release of all of that grief and guilt that surely was penned up inside of Gabriel's beautiful soul for far too long. The tears he saw reassured him and he continued with his counsel.

"I know you feel burdened and weighed down by Benjamin's death. I know you think of yourself and have always thought of yourself as the little brother of Benjamin Loveman, the poor nigger who was lynched when he was farming late one night, farming land he loved but did not even own."

David crossed his arms and shifted his weight as he spoke.

"You know some folks right here in these Quarters figured Benjamin brought it on himself because he was crazy enough to work as hard as he did knowing that more than likely he would never see a profit from his work. That no matter how good the crop, how ample the harvest, the Loveman's would always end up in the red. Mr. Peterson runs the numbers and Mr. Peterson owns the farm. So it don't take a smart mind to know we ain't gone never pay him off. Those folks think that Benjamin must have been too dumb, too gullible to know that. That surely he labored away through the nights because he thought he could work his family out of their debt to Mr. Peterson. They even laughed at him for taking such a notion. But they were wrong, Gabriel. Flat out and miserably wrong. Benjamin never got in his head that he would work so hard and so good that he would eventually pay old evil Robert Peterson off. As matter of fact, long ago, before even your mother and father were willing to admit it, before I would even come to terms with it myself, Benjamin accepted our plight here on this God-forsaken farm."

As he reflected on the amazing character of his elder nephew, David's heart opened up and for the first time in a long time, he allowed himself to enjoy his memories of his golden boy lost. He wanted Gabriel to somehow find a way to do the same, to somehow begin the balancing act of appreciating Benjamin's life and mourning his untimely death. David knew in his heart that Gabriel was tormented by his big brother's treacherous demise, as well as by a restless resignation that his own life would waste away there on the plantation he loathed. Perhaps, David could ease the torment just a bit by reminding Gabriel just how much Benjamin had loved his homeland. Moving around to the side of Gabriel so that he could lean against the tree and rest his tired, achy back, David steadied himself by placing one hand on Gabriel's shoulder. As he tilted his head toward the last hint of sunlight, David reflected on Benjamin's love for life.

"When he was just a young boy, he decided that he would farm this land just for the sake of farming, that he would labor for love's sake and nothing else. That is why he was so happy. That's why he sang with so much joy in his voice. I always said he had laughter in his heart. He knew that Robert Peterson was in the business of oppressing those who live here and who work themselves to death here, all the while waiting for him to do the right thing or for him to die and for the books to somehow add up to what equals right. As far as your brother was concerned, he wasn't working to pay off a debt to no rich white man so our family could get the title to the land, because, to him, there was really no such thing as land ownership. In his mind, this land no more rightfully belonged to Robert Peterson than it did to him or any of us. A long, long time ago, Benjamin made up in his head that that owning land is a crazy notion, a feeble idea that rests in the minds of white men and he put it in his own mind to never to want to own this land, to only use and appreciate the earth, experience and cultivate the ground. And that is why, as horrible as his death was, I know he died a happy man."

David stopped talking in order to catch his breath and to allow a little time for Gabriel to absorb the depth of what he had just said, while he gathered the strength to make the final and most necessary point to his nephew, who he loved as if he were his own child.

"His death was horrible. Ain't much more I can say about the way our boy died, but you need to understand Gabriel, that Benjamin, when he died, well, he was free. He wasn't living to meet nobody's needs but his own. He damn sure wasn't trying to pay Robert Peterson off. He didn't think that man could give him nothing or take nothing away from him. He was free, more than anybody I ever knew. That's why we loved him so and that is why we miss him, all day every day. When we had him with us, when he was around,we knew what free was like. That is what he gave us. He showed us that free is singing if you have the gift of song. Free is farming if you have a way with the land and got a special knack for making things grow. Free is doing what you do not so you can own something, but simply because you are able to do it."

As Gabriel returned his gaze back to the shaded ground beneath his feet, his Uncle David went on to make what would be his final comment on the matter at hand.

"When you think about it, and believe me boy, I do know how much you been thinking about things, maybe that's how you ought to look at your own life, Gabriel. Stop trying to own it. Stop trying to decide what to do with it. And furthermore stop trying to live your brother's life. You don't honor him by doing so. You want to honor

Benjamin? If that is what you really want to do, then stop trying so damn hard. Period. Stop deciding. Dammit, stop thinking and just live, Gabriel. Live doing what you love to do. Live life hoping and dreaming and making those dreams come true. If you are going to honor your brother, stop thinking about, crying over, and trying to make up for his death. You ain't nothing like your brother, boy. That little ant you just stepped on a minute ago is more like your brother than you are because they are both dead. Whatever they were going to do on this earth already been done. You on the other hand got to get busy living. You don't owe us nothing, son. Even if you somehow came to farm as good as he did. Even if you opened your mouth and sang his favorite song as well as he sang it when he was among the living, even if you were able to harvest the crop that toppled the Loveman's out of debt and gave us that flimsy piece of paper declaring us the owners of that property, we still would miss Benjamin. That hole in our hearts ain't gone never be filled. Only thing you do is make another one because when we see you trying so hard to live your big brother's life, well then we got to mourn you, too. If you ain't gone live your life Gabriel, the one the good Lord has laid out just for you, then you just about as dead as your brother and as lifeless as that ant underneath your foot."

The night had begun to creep in and so Gabriel could barely see, only hear the slow, methodical steps as his uncle hobbled back up the path toward the cabin, leaving him alone and in the dark to consider what had been said and to wipe away his tears.

Chapter Eleven

COWARDS AND CONSEQUENCES

Martha's favorite time of the day in the summer was late after-noon, the time of day when the heat is hot enough to be soothing but settled enough for one to endure and actually enjoy a southern summer day. The few hours just before sunset was the time of day when she found herself most reflective about her life. She loved to open the school doors and windows, while she cleaned and organized her tiny academy in preparation for the next day's session and she would go about her afternoon routine with the background noise of the small children of the Quarters playing nearby. Their squeals of delight and glee, along with the hum of the chatter or the singing of the laborers as they headed home from the field was a therapeutic reminder to her that she had done the right things years ago when she made her fateful decision to remain in the South and on the Peterson Plantation. The sounds of the Quarters during the evening dusk brought a certain soothing to her soul, an air of peace-fulness to her life. Until recently, the closing of the day was also the time she spent anticipating Gabriel's arrival for his evening study session. For the past few years, Martha has spent most of her evenings with her most ardent, most gifted student, Gabriel Loveman. He had initially began private evening study sessions with her just so she could expose him to more advanced subjects and academic topics without overwhelming or intimidating her other students. Meeting with Gabriel, night after night, after long days in the classroom that sweltered with heat in the summertime and chilled bones in the winter, was her heart's delight and Martha never felt burdened by the extra time and effort that she spent teaching Gabriel Loveman. Their nights of study together was her investment in his future, a future that she was convinced could be great and notable.

When tragedy struck the Loveman family and Gabriel was forced out of the classroom and into the labor field for the sake of his family's survival on the plantation, Martha extended their night studies by two more hours and required Gabriel to work another hour on his own when he returned to his family's cabin each night. She knew that her doing so would compromise the amount of much needed rest he would get before returning to the treacherous work the next day's field labor would require, but she also knew that this sacrifice was necessary. Gabriel's successful end would justify any weariness, any exhaustion either of them experienced along the way, for she was determined that his life would be spent in a profession and not on a field and she became dogged in her mission to get him away from any and everything associated with the Peterson Plantation. For those who said she was doing too much, giving too much of her own time and wearing herself out, she always responded with the same declaration. "I could never do too much for Gabriel."

Behind those words, though, were thoughts much too complex and far too sensitive to explain. There was no way she could simplify the complexity of her connection with Gabriel, no way that she could explain that he was more, much more than a pet project or a fascination, even. There was absolutely no way, in one conversation, Martha could make sense of what took her years to comprehend and understand, which was that by doing all she could do to prepare Gabriel for a life beyond the Peterson Plantation, she was also redeeming her own self, forgiving herself and freeing herself from the choices, the painful choices of her past.

She knew that there was one conversation she had to have, one that she could not avoid, if she was going to truly help Gabriel Loveman. Not having that conversation would mean every single second of time she spent teaching and encouraging Gabriel would be wasted, a useless feat that bore little, if any, results. The time had come for her to have the one conversation she had dreaded nearly all of her adult years. The time was upon her and Gabriel's plight depended on her courage, on her honesty, and her vulnerability. Only for Gabriel's sake could she imagine being so brave, displaying such a sensitive truth and placing herself at such high risk for an emotional harm that almost matched the risk of physical harm Gabriel faced if he took action on his acceptance letter. Thinking about it all, Martha couldn't help but to chuckle. Seeing as how the two of them had conspired to accomplish all the tasks that led to his receipt of the letter, perhaps it made sense that she shared his risk. After all, she had been the one who made it her business to do more than just accept Gabriel's genius, she had done all she could to enrich, guide, protect and, yes, purpose his brilliance by preparing him for an education beyond that which she could provide and he could obtain anywhere close to the place he called home. She had planted the seed in his mind, established the zany notion that he could and should go away to a school of higher learning and build a future that was better suited for his gifts and talents. Martha was the one who convinced Gabriel, time and time again, that all of of his sacrifices and all of his hard work and commitment would pay off and that his future compelled his going the extra mile for the sake of his studies, that what he could do and what he had to offer the world deserved every bit of his seriousness and focus. She had pushed and, some days, she had even pried, days when he was exhausted from the field's demands or weary from life's tortuous treatment of him and his loved ones. And

Gabriel had relented, like no other child or any other person she had ever known would have. He had trusted her with his genius and with his stamina and determination. He had done all that she had asked of him, all the while knowing how much of an uphill battle he faced at the mere thought of a young man in his situation going to college. As unusual and cruel of a reality being a black genius on a southern plantation was, Gabriel had placed his life on the line by applying and receiving the letter of acceptance. The least she could do was place her life there alongside his to make sure that he more than received the letter. If she was to be any good for him and for herself, Martha had to make sure that letter came to life. No matter how high the risk, she had to do any and everything she could to make Gabriel's leaving possible. Then the decision would truly be his to make, freely and without the weight of wickedness, poverty and oppression. She owed him that much and the time had come for her to do what she had long known she would have to do, if she really wanted to support her precious, beloved student. After sitting and thinking for a while and then praying even longer, Martha stood up from her old raggedy desk, dusted her skirt, tied a bonnet over her stark red hair and headed up to the huge house atop the hill to go and have a long, overdue conversation with her twin brother, Robert.

For the first few years after the death of his older brother, Robert Peterson did everything he could to prove to his father that he was worthy of the love and trust that had so freely been bestowed upon the firstborn and expected heir to the Peterson Plantation. Initially, he did so by simply pretending to be Richard, Jr. and by emulating everything he knew about his brother. He took on Richard Jr.'s persona and became cocky and arrogant. He went from being an introvert to an extrovert, albeit not a very friendly one. He dressed in his brother's clothes, wore his brother's boots, and carried his brother's watch. He even took his brother's seat at the weekly poker game played by the young men who were all considered to be "the next in line" for ownership of the most prosperous farmlands in the state. They were the sons of notable politicians, judges, and successful business owners and Robert Peterson took his brother's place at the card table and he took on his brother's role in the secret society made up of young white men only. The leaders of the society just so happened to be the same poker players he gambled with every week, so there was hardly any indication as to when the card game ended and the secret society meeting began, except the secret society and its mission called for the adorning of special attire, special robes and and when Robert Peterson dressed for meetings and missions it was Richard Jr.'s uniform he wore.

Robert Peterson even went so far as to marry the girl his brother was courting before he died, a girl most would have considered plain except she was made quite attractive by her family's status and her father's wealth. Nancy Jackson Peterson was a typical southern belle, who had more money than she did beauty and charm. She came from a family with ties so deeply rooted that the State in which they lived bore her surname. Robert Peterson married her for one reason only and that was to please his grieving father.

Despite his constant display of honor and regard for his dearly departed sibling, despite his best effort to fill his shoes, Robert Peterson never received the recognition, the acknowledgement, even, from the father that he so desperately wanted to make proud. That his father seemed oblivious to him even without his brother's presence to overshadow him broke what little heart Robert Peterson ever had and as the years passed, he became driven by his bitterness and hatred for the man he once so desperately loved. He then lived life to prove the senior Richard Peterson a fool for failing to see the glory in his second son and as the Peterson Plantation grew in wealth and portion and as the patriarch became older and more frail, Robert Peterson openly ridiculed him as a mediocre farmer and businessman and publicly regarded him as nothing more than a nuisance he tolerated out of respect for tradition. When Richard Peterson, Sr. died, the great fanfare funeral that his youngest son orchestrated was not in tribute to a beloved father by a grieving son, but rather was a display to all those who knew them both of the influence, esteem, and financial success Robert Peterson had accomplished since taking over the family business. Grief played no part in the matter, for Robert Peterson had not been saddened at all by his father's passing. As a matter of fact, he was elated at the thought of finally having the family assets all to himself and he was ecstatic at the thought of never having to answer to or care for the old man ever again. Robert Peterson was glad his father was dead and he buried his father without the shedding of so much as a single tear. What others thought of as a dignified approach to bereavement was actually a display of disregard, discontent and relief that he was the remaining heir to the Peterson Plantation. There were no other brothers to contend with for power, no siblings at all who would lay claim to his inheritance. The piling of the last heap of dirt on his father's grave solidified Robert Peterson's status as owner of all his father assets, assets that were generated with the thought they would be passed down to Richard Jr., for he was the oldest, the heir apparent and his father's pride and joy. His sudden, tragic death years before had left a void in the elder Peterson's life and when Robert realized that nothing he did would ever fill that void, he became embittered toward his father and resentful of his constant grieving over the loss his beloved namesake. Up until Robert's realization of the vast difference in his father's feelings for him and those he felt for Richard Jr. and the realization that he would never be able to do anything to make up that difference, even though his brother was dead and gone, Robert Peterson had lived life relentlessly trying to gain approval. All he did, he did for to accomplish the love and acceptance of those close to him. He had done unspeakable things, horrible things for the sake of his father's and his brother's love. Still, the younger Richard Peterson had died without actually verbalizing his acceptance of little brother and their father, Richard Sr., had died without ever declaring love and acceptance of his youngest son.

A few years after Richard died, when his father was too old and too sick to protest or do anything thing about it, Robert Peterson had stopped living for the sake of his family's love and had begun to work and live solely for the appeasement of himself, purely for the sake of his own personal satisfaction. His father's death left him as the last Peterson man alive and he was glad to have the family empire all to himself. With them both gone, all of his decisions and actions were completely self-centered and were solely for his satisfaction.

He hadn't always been mean and wicked. He was born a child of pleasant nature, wide-eyed and curious. Yet, from the day he was born, he was overshadowed by his senior sibling. The yearning for acceptance and love from his father and his older brother, who seemed to bask in their father's pride, intensified with his age and by the time he was twelve, nothing was more important to him than gaining their approval. The older he got the more determined he was to show them, to prove to them that he was worthy of the kind of accreditation that was given to white men in the South, who were rich and who lived life knowing that they were superior to everyone else, including their wives and children. More than that, they were superior to those who had less wealth, meaning the wealthier you were, the more respect and admiration you were due. White folks who were less fortunate consented to this social approach, which is why the Peterson family was so well-known and well respected. Most importantly, as a notable white man in the south, you stood incredibly superior to the people of color, who just a few decades before had actually been slaves. By the time Robert Peterson was coming of age, slaves had been "freed," at least on paper. However, the ways of the South were holding hard and fast and his family's farming operation was functional and productive only because of their dependence on an unpaid labor force. In what some considered an act of genius, his father had somehow convinced the former slaves owned by the Petersons that they were free and that his provision of food, clothing and shelter was actually his way of paying them for the same work they performed when they were enslaved. The food, clothing and housing were the same as what had been provided to the slaves of the Peterson Plantation, the only difference being Old Man Peterson put a price tag on the provisions and "graciously" allowed the former slaves and then their children and grandchildren to work off the debt they owed him for his "generosity." The so-called genius aspect of his employer-employee arrangement was his issuance of deeds to each family that lived in the area of the Peterson Plantation known as the Quarters. Old Man Peterson had explained that any man who received a deed would only become a landowner upon the payment of the debt owed to him or his heirs, whenever the debt was finally paid. In truth, final payment was a far-fetched idea given the fact the Petersons controlled the rates for wage, food prices, lodging fees and clothing costs. Somehow, some way, the cost of living expenses always overrode the actual earnings of the Peterson field laborers and year, after year, they found themselves more indebted to the Peterson family and farther away from land ownership.

Though the financial arrangement was the brainstorm of his father, Robert Peterson had expounded on the idea and by the summer of Gabriel's dilemma, not only were the tenants of the Quarters beholden to his family's empire, many of the poor white residents of Chester County were also employees of the Peterson Plantation, who endured the shameful, despicable plight of working alongside the people they commonly referred to as "nigras." Though the pay was meager, the white field laborers and farm hands were, still, actually paid tangible money, although they had to turn right around and hand most of their earnings right back over to pay for rent, as well as food and supplies purchased on credit from the General Store, which was also owned by Robert Peterson. That they actually were paid their wages rather than merely being shown a ledger that calculated debt from week to week, gave them a sense of distinction and pride in the fact that were white people, pitiful and pathetically poor but, still, white in color. In reality, they, too, were merely assets of the Peterson estate and just as readily disposable as the "nigras" they deplored.

By the time Richard Peterson, Sr. died, his youngest son was living life satisfied with his awareness that he had surpassed both his father and his dead brother in the worldly means of wealth and social status. More than money and economic power, though, Robert Peterson was most proud of his ability to be and to act more hateful than any of his closest male kin. He lived his life constantly proving to himself that the day he had failed to earn the acceptance and approval of his father and brother was last day as a weak-hearted man. From that day forward, whether the matter involved a beating, rape or murder, every act of hatred on his part sourced Robert Peterson's pride in his ability to be heartless. There was no limit to his evilness and, without conscience, he would orchestrate and even personally perform horrendous acts in order to display his disdain toward the people of color who lived and worked on his property and he was especially prepared to use violence to address any effort on Gabriel Loveman's part to act on a college acceptance letter. He had killed niggers for much more meaningless transgressions. Killing Gabriel and the entire Loveman family was something he was prepared to do in order to remind everyone else in the Quarters that as far as he was concerned, there was no such thing as a genius nigger and, more importantly, no such freedom on their part to ever leave the Peterson Plantation.

Life has a funny way of being the same, day after day, until the day everything changes. Over the course of a week, when she had been confronted by Rosalee Loveman, undergone her usual engagement with her precious students, delved into the deepest layers of her memory to reveal her truth to Ella, ventured into the town she hardly ever frequented, for a most necessary meeting and to arrange an urgent telegraphed message, up until the eve when she found herself marching up the steps of the mansion that housed her childhood, Martha Peterson's life had changed tremendously. She would never be the same. No matter what occurred, no matter the outcome of the instances of her evening, her life had changed forever.

As Martha made her way toward the grand house she had once called home, she realized how unfamiliar she had become with her family's estate. As the only daughter of one of the wealthiest men in the State, from the time she was born, Martha was doted on by her mother and father. They spared no expense adorning their only daughter, who, by all accounts, was a remarkably beautiful child. As a young southern belle and heir to the Peterson Plantation, she became one of the most sought after young ladies of her generation and she beheld all the makings of a life desired by most every southern white woman. She was lovely, smart and held a birthright to one of the grandest estates of the South, an estate she denied herself and relinquished to her twin brother in exchange for his permission of the establishment and continued operation her school. As she approached her childhood home, Martha was reminded of her family's wealth and power and the stronghold her brother held over most residents of Chester County. The pedigree of the Peterson family was ranked highest among their kind because, unlike most rich families that had built their wealth using slave labor, the men in the Peterson clan did not partake in sexual relations with the women they considered property or financial assets. Robert Peterson's great grandfather and grandfather had not slept with their slaves and his father had not slept with his "sharecroppers." Thus, the Peterson's bloodline was purely white and the family name did not bear the blemish of any kinship with mulatoos, quadroons or octoroons. White purity was coveted and highly esteemed, for very few southern families could honestly make such a distinguishable proclamation. Robert Peterson had expanded his family's dynasty and had heightened his own social status even more when he married a woman whose family had also maintained a purely white family lineage.

As the wife of one of the wealthiest plantation owners in the South and the daughter of one of the richest men in the State, Martha's sister-in-law, Nancy Peterson was considered by most who knew her to be the quintessential southern matron. In her youthful years, her coloration was ideal, for then, her skin was pale and her long hair blond in color. Furthermore, she was petite in stature and in character she presented the socially acceptable manner of politeness blended with a snide, contrary demeanor. Still, despite her family's reputation, her husband's wealth and her placement in high southern society, Nancy Peterson was a miserable woman. When she was just a young lady, shortly after her introduction into society, her misery had been triggered when her beau died suddenly in horse-riding accident. as she had been happily engaged to Richard Peterson, Jr., the heir apparent to the Peterson Plantation. Her marriage to his younger and far less handsome brother, Robert, was a resignation on her part to the decision made by their fathers who were determined to preserve the purity of both families' bloodlines. As the years progressed and as he succeeded in his expansion of his family's empire, her husband became more and more brutal and insolent as a man and as a spouse. Their marriage was mostly void of both intimacy and compassion and they coexisted much more than they acted as a marital couple. Her misery in her marriage was compounded even more by their inability to conceive children. Nancy Peterson had never been pregnant and the recurring argument between her and her husband was rooted in exactly who was to blame for her barrenness. He thought of her as useless and damaged. She was convinced he was as infertile as he was evil. Both of their fathers had died gravely disappointed that their arrangement had extended the wealth of their estates but had failed to expand their pure bloodlines to any grandchildren.

Though Nancy Peterson publicly bore the face of the typical smug and satisfied southern wife, privately, she simply was an unhappy

169

woman who existed more than she actually lived a life with any depth. Although she would never admit her innermost thoughts out loud, she deeply envied Martha, the maiden lady who lived alone on the edge of her family's property and who spent her days with purpose, even if that purpose was merely teaching nigger children. Martha, too, was childless, but at least she did not have to share her life with a brute monster of a man and at least she had something to look forward to each day. Of course, Nancy Peterson would never divulge her true sentiment about her life and her marriage to anyone. With the exception of not having any children and thus any immediate heirs to the estate she shared with her husband, as far as her society was concerned, Nancy Peterson lived the life that was dreamed of by most other white people in the South and so she suffered in the manner she and everyone in her society thought best to so suffer, which was silently.

She was sitting on her front porch indulging herself one of the several mint juleps she consumed on a daily basis, when Martha, the maiden school teacher, arrived on the porch steps. The two women had never forged a relationship and hardly knew one another, personally, though Nancy Peterson knew enough to know she was not the subject of the teacher's visit. She immediately stood and opened her front door, welcoming Martha inside in the same fashion most southern wives acknowledged and ushered guests into their homes, with a slight nod and a polite, curt greeting. After instructing one of the house servants to inform her husband of his awaiting guest, she returned to her front porch, her mint julep and her silence.

∽

"Well now, Martha!" Robert Peterson exclaimed. "What a surprise! What brings you to my door?"

For almost three decades the Peterson twins, Martha and Robert, had cohabitated on the estate they jointly owned. Martha deliberately kept her distance from her brother and from the community that so greatly revered her family name. Whenever she saw her brother, the passing was brief and any exchange, if any at all, was one of few words that conveyed hardly any thought or sentiment. Seeing him up close and face-to-face, Martha could not help but notice how hateful her twin brother physically appeared. The bearings of his tortured soul seemed to have taken charge of his facial features, as well as his physique. On sight, one would have assumed he was her father more so than her sibling, for his hatred had aged him beyond his years. The sight of him in such close proximity stirred unexpected emotions and Martha was taken aback by what felt like a sharp sadness for the man with whom she once held so close a connection. The day she lost Hannah she had lost him, too, and the man appearing before her was a stranger, someone who was nothing like the young lad who had sacrificed his goodness for the lost cause of a father's love and an older brother's acceptance.

"Are you really all that surprised, Robert? Surely, you know why I am here."

If Martha didn't know him better, she would have believed the hint of bewilderment in Robert's voice, when he replied.

"No. Can't say I do. I can't imagine what would entice you to visit with me, Martha, seeing how you hardly ever do. And when you do grace us with your presence, seems you and me, always find ourselves at odds for some reason or another."

Stopping to ponder for a moment, Robert Peterson seemed amused with himself when he continued to speak.

"As a matter of fact, as much as you keep to yourself, away from me and everyone else who knows you, I'm not only surprised that you've made your way to the house today. Hell. I'm surprised you're still around these parts at all. You got no husband, got no friends. All you have is that little shack of yours you call a school and I can't think of anything more useless on this farm that that. And seeing how you've made no effort to keep in touch with me, except when you want something of course, I declare, I am just about at my wits end as to why you remain here at all."

Clearly, from his tone and his demeanor, Robert's words were not born of fresh thoughts and he was just seizing the opportunity to say exactly how he felt about his sister for most of their adult lives. Martha was not short of a reply. Indeed, what she had to say to Robert had also been years in formation and she knew in her heart of hearts she could no longer withhold her feelings about him, their connection and her life on Peterson Plantation.

"For years, I have convinced myself that I stayed here, that I gave up the wonderful life I could have had as a wife and a mother simply because, more than anything else, I wanted to help those people who live in the Quarters and labor in those fields. And that is true. I have always wanted to help them and to serve them, but here lately, with everything that has been going on with Gabriel this summer, I have had to really, truthfully consider why I did not leave this place years ago, when I had the chance."

Martha felt the need to straighten her back and look at the man before her pointedly, eye to eye. Drawing a deep breath, her voice was more resigned when she spoke again.

"I wish I could say that I came to this realization on my own. I suppose that if I had ever taken the time, if I had ever mustered the courage to do so, I would have been honest with myself a long time ago. That kind of courage isn't natural for me though, any more than courage is natural for you, but after my visit with Rosalee, I've decided to borrow a bit of her strength and so I am here, standing in front of you, the brother I've tried with all my might to distance myself from, the man I have both despised and feared for so long, I don't even remember what it feels like to be his kin. Robert, I swear. I really don't. And yet, we are kindred spirits. Are we not the closest of kin? I mean, it can't get any closer than the sharing of a womb. And as hard as it is to admit to myself and even harder to stand before you and say this, but the truth is, I stayed here, in large part, for you.

I've lived here on the edge of this estate, right there where privilege stops and persecution begins, right there in a little lonely house aside my raggedy, little school, there where I don't belong to the society you rule and there where I am tolerated but not quite accepted by those folks who live in the Quarters, there alone, all by myself – for you. Deep down I've always known that but I never had the courage to accept that just as much as I've lived here all these years so that I could be at peace with myself and to help all of those beautiful children, I've remained here because of you."

Robert Peterson was baffled by his twin sister's candor but still he quickly replied to her admission.

"You hate me. Let's neither of us pretend like you don't." he said, sneering his nose as he continued with his chide. "So how in the hell do you figure your staying here, dwelling amongst a bunch of niggers, teaching 'em things they don't need to know and won't ever use- how in the world do you figure that's on account of me?"

For a conversation that was years in the making, the exchange between Robert and Martha, brother to sister, twin to twin, had become a rapid fire of retorts. When she spoke again, Martha did not mince her words. She knew she had far more to gain than she did to lose by being forthright with her brother.

"Yes. You are right, Robert. I do hate you. I hate the sight of you. I know who you are and I know how you feel about the people who break their backs day in and day out, working in your fields. And I know of the senseless acts, of all the cruelty you've committed against them for God knows how long. And I hate the man that you are and I hate all of the hurt you've caused, without any regret and no shame, it seems."

Martha could hear the nervousness returning to her voice and so she paused. She knew she had to show no sign of feeling intimidated. Her brother preyed upon fear and if he sensed that she was not ready to handle his reaction to what she had come to say, at the very least, he would dismiss her without regard for her demand. She couldn't even allow herself to think about the worst case scenario. Taking in a long breath to regain her composure, Martha continued, her voice loud and defiant.

"For years, I have ignored my hatred of you as much as possible and preoccupied myself otherwise just trying in large part not to deal with my feelings for you- not because you don't deserve my hatred. You do. The hard cold truth, what I have busied myself trying to escape all these years, is the fact that as much as I hate you, there is a part of me, the part I cannot disconnect from, no matter how hard I try, that still loves you."

Drawing breath again as she carefully considered her next words, Martha gazed deeply into the cold, almost lifeless eyes of the man standing before her, the brother she knew so well and at the same time hardly recognized at all.

"We entered this world together. And though I make every effort to stay away from you and your wicked ways, I will always feel bonded to you or so it seems. For that very reason, my hatred for you has driven me from the world I knew so long ago. There was no way I could survive here, hating you the way I do, for surely I would have lived life hating myself, despising the part of me that is drawn to you, just as much as I despise you and this evil community, this shameful and disgraceful life that you and your so-called friends live. I was so afraid that if I didn't separate myself from this society, I would lose that part of me that knows, believes so very much that everything about our upbringing and manner of living is wrong, more than wrong, it is damning. I have been so afraid of becoming like you I haven't ever given way to truly being myself. The bond of being your twin, that bond has been the source of a fear that up until now has just about controlled my whole life."

Robert Peterson's impatience became clear as he pointed his finger toward the front door and interrupted her once again.

"What in the hell are you talking about? You're talking as if I care at all about what you think! Well, I don't so whatever led you to trot your little high and mighty self up the pathway to my house, I suggest you get over it and get your ass back down there with the rest of the good for nothings!"

Surprisingly to both of them, his outburst had absolutely no effect on Martha and she spoke next with stark deliberation.

"You know exactly what I am talking about and I've only just begun. I will finish what I have to say to you, though Robert. I've come here today to have my say and I will. If it kills me...."

Slowing her speech, Martha shifted her weight slightly to better meet her brother's eye level. She needed him to fully register her determination and her resolve.

"If you kill me, so be it. But I will have my say today. And I suggest you remember that this here plantation is not really just yours, now is it? So don't tell me to get out. I'll get out when I've had my say."

There was a long pause as Martha waited to see what Robert would do next. When he sat down in the high back parlor chair against the wall of the long hallway where they were standing, she couldn't help but feel a renewed sense of confidence. She only had to hint at her claim to his wealth and he was already about knocked off his feet. She crossed her arms and braced herself for what was to be the most important thing she had ever said her whole life long. With a straight back and tilted chin, she began to make the point that was the main reason for her visit that day.

"I've been so worried that being your twin automatically meant that I was made up of the same evil, the same badness that consumes you and your entire way of being that I somehow lost myself, trying so hard to be and live the opposite of you. But I've had it. I should have had enough long ago and especially before Benjamin was killed."

Martha paused again before stating the realization that had just come to her mind.

"No. I should have had it when you hurt Hanna!"

By bringing up Hanna's name and referencing her twin brother's youthful plunge into the darkness of violence and bigotry, Martha ignited a fury in Robert Peterson that is difficult for most human beings to even imagine. But Martha had imagined his reaction. She had considered his likely response when she had made up her mind to fight for Gabriel. She knew how her brother would respond and she was prepared to do whatever was necessary to deal with the ramifications that could follow the confrontation with him. So even when he hopped to his feet upon hearing Hannah's name, even as he hovered over her with his nostrils flared and his eyes reddened in anger, Martha did not break. She kept talking. She knew that if she paused, if she hesitated for even a sparse second or two, her surge of confidence would likely dwindle, so she braced herself sturdily and soundly spoke the words flowing from her heart.

"Robert, everyone who knows you fears you. And they should. Every since the day you tried to earn the love of Father and Richard, Jr. by hurting Hanna, you have been a pretty pathetic person, one monster of a man, a most despicable and heartless human being. At the time that it happened, I didn't understand how you could do such a thing. I thought you loved her same as I did. But I guess even then you suffered from the same emptiness you still suffer from now as you stand here looking as if you want nothing less than to kill me, your own flesh and blood for daring to say these things to you. I suppose Hanna herself saw the same look the day you dragged that poor girl into the woods, raped her and then tried to kill her, all for the sake of some twisted and perverted love from a father and a brother who, like you, Robert, never really had any real love to give. The monster in you awoke that day and you have been destroying and killing ever since. And if you don't think you actually succeeding in killing Hanna that day, you are just as stupid as you are mean. Yeah. Sure. Physically she survived, but she's been nothing more than a shell of a human since the boy she thought was her friend stole her innocence and tried to take her life. Hanna is the first of all the human debris left behind from your evilness and your hatred of anyone who doesn't look like you. As sure as I stand here, you killed her, killed almost every part of who she was before that terrible day. She's never been the same. She was a beautiful, happy girl who loved us, Robert. And you killed her. Just like you killed Benjamin."

Robert Peterson had become completely unnerved by his sister's candor. Not one to easily allow others to become aware when he was nervous or upset, Robert rocked back on his feet and with a hint of glee and then disrupted what he considered to be a crazed rant by a pitiful and lonely woman.

"Oh, well, hell, Martha! I suspect, let you tell it, I am responsible for every dead nigger within a hundred miles of this house!"

Martha remained unshaken. As a matter of fact, his mockery only fueled her anger and strengthened her composure.

"I don't know," she said with conviction. "But it wouldn't surprise me."

"Well this may come as a surprise to you Miss High and Mighty! But I ain't the one that killed Benjamin. Didn't do me no good to off him. That was one of the best field hands I had. Most of 'em, including that little pet of yours, ain't worth shit."

His casual manner while referring to such a horrendous killing should have shocked Martha but she wasn't surprised. The longer she stood before him the smaller of a man he became and Martha felt braver than she had ever felt in her entire life. The more she considered exactly the kind of person her twin brother was the more she felt the need to reveal to him her exact thoughts about their matters of difference.

"You did kill him. Maybe not with your own hands. I don't know if you yourself gave the order that he be killed or if you just made way for the ones who were after him for so long to be able to murder that poor boy without fear of any retaliation from you. Everybody who knows you knows there is no way it would have happened if you weren't completely fine with it. I know it and the Lovemans know it. And if Gabriel had any doubt, well, you took care of that the day you gave him his letter, now didn't you?"

Robert Peterson was conflicted. He was both confused and enraged by his sister's outburst and sudden display of courage. He had lived for so many years hardly having to consider anything about her at all. The only time she ever contacted him, it seemed, was out of what he considered her pitiful effort to educate or advocate for a bunch of damn near worthless niggers. For so long, he had used her guilt and her shame against her. He knew why she tried so hard to keep a distance not just from him but from everything about the life he lived. As long as she lived in isolation, keeping only to herself and the niggers she loved so much, he was able to run his southern empire without having to even consider his twin's legal status. She seemed satisfied with her little house and her little school and her life on her own. He hardly ever saw her and when he did, hardly a word was uttered between them. On this day, she had spoken to him more than all their days put together. As she stood before him, looking as if she was not only disgusted by him but also as if she pitied him, Robert's blood began to boil with fury. Realizing that she truly thought more of the Lovemans than she did her own flesh and blood was infuriating and the thought of her having such a close relationship with Gabriel triggered another angry outburst.

"I suppose your little pet nigger tells you everything, huh? Well I don't give a damn what that letter says and I could care even less how smart he is, he ain't nothing to me but a nigger, a darky fit only for my field!"

Martha remained unmoved.

"You can call him all the names you want to but you and I both know that Gabriel Loveman is more of a man than you will ever be. As a matter of fact, Robert, I don't consider you a man at all. I know you think you are-because you have money and power. But every-thing you have, you have gotten out of fear. Sure people do business with you and sure, Robert, you live in a grand house and hold grand affairs along with your esteemed southern belle of a wife. And sure, all of white society reveres you. You solicit and people respond. You beckon and they arrive. Yes, indeed."

Gazing deeply into her brother's eyes, Martha spoke what she felt may be her final words to him ever.

"People respond to you not because they love or respect you. They don't. They do you fear you, though. And I know you don't give a damn about being loved. You lost any need for that the second you realized that you would never truly be valued or admired by Father or Richard, Jr. But, somehow, you have convinced yourself that people respect you, that you are the example of success and aspiration, that every white man wishes he could be you, strives to be just like you, rich, influential and the epitome of power and respect. Except that you aren't respected Robert. You are feared. And there is a huge difference between the two. People do what you demand because they know that if they don't, you won't hesitate to take their lives or the lives of their loved ones. They are afraid of you. They know that you kill without conscience. That you lack compassion and are without a soul. They know you place very little or no value on the lives of others. What they don't know, what is unimaginable to most everyone who knows you Robert Peterson is that deep down you don't even really, truly value yourself. People have no idea that this great and powerful man that they fear so much is really the smallest human being they'll probably ever know. Nobody knows that your soul disappeared along with Hanna that day in the woods so long ago."

The words Martha spoke struck Robert to the core and as she continued, he backed away from her slowly and sat, again, in the high back chair, thankful for the support for his legs seemed ready to give way at any second. He had not allowed himself to revisit the day that had changed his life. Deep down he knew that if he ever lingered on the memory for more than a few seconds, he just might connect with his conscience, a conscience that would reveal his shame, his loneliness, and his guilt. Rather than face his wrong, Robert had decided to justify his actions. Because he hurt Hannah, the little girl he once loved so dearly, he would not hesitate to hurt anyone, he decided that day long ago. The only other option would be to acknowledge those things about himself that enabled him to hurt others and that he could not, would not live with. Looking at the sister who, upon careful gaze, resembled him so greatly and hearing her say the things he would never allow his own conscience to examine was more than overwhelming. Bewildered and spent, Robert bent his head as Martha shared with him her innermost thoughts about him and the way he had chosen to live his life.

"If only everyone knew how very little you left with the day you came out of those woods- where you not only left Hannah's life hanging in the balance, but where you also left any good you had in you behind. You came out of those woods that day void of love, void of hope and just about every life you have touched since then has suffered for it. And for what, Robert? The love for two other evil pitiful and pathetic men who never returned that love to you? For what? This large life you live in this large house on this large planta-tion with a wife who is so embittered by the ways of her world that she's barren of children and an absolute bore to all who know her? For what? The honor and respect of being at the helm of the wealth-iest and so-called purest estate amongst your kind? Hmph."

Martha had become indignant in her delivery. She hadn't known exactly what she was going to say to her brother to state her deter-mination and her support of Gabriel, but the more she talked, the safer she felt. There she was standing before and challenging the most treacherous person she had ever known and the more she spoke her truth, the more she relayed to him just what she thought of him, the more resound and secure she felt. She knew there was no turning back anyway. And as much as Robert was visibly shaken by what she was saying, Martha still knew that at any given moment he was capable of killing her and would not hesitate to do so with his bare hands. Somehow, some way, Martha had become more afraid of not having her say, of not being her whole and complete self than she was of what her brother could do to her. Though she had her life to lose by challenging him the way she was, she also had her life to gain, her life and so much more by taking her stand against him.

"Well, Robert," Martha said emphatically, boldly. "The wealth is not all yours, now is it? Those fields belong to the both of us, equally and nothing you can do will change that. If you could have, you would have by now. Every time you add on to this estate, every time you purchase so much as a foot of grass, you do so knowing that you increase an estate that belongs to the both of us. Our Father never had much faith in you, no matter how hard you tried to earn his love and respect. He died knowing I had no husband and still he left this place to us jointly, equally. He knew I wanted no part of it and still he left it in such a way that I could state my claim whenever I so decided. Had Richard Jr. outlived him, do you think Father would have left this place to the three of us equally, jointly? Of course, he wouldn't have. But when Richard died, so did Father's concern over whatever would happen to the Peterson Plantation after he was gone. Nothing you did mattered to him and if you didn't know that by the way he treated you, he certainly made sure you knew it by the way he left the place to the both us. I own this place just as much as you do and though I don't want it, I will stake my claim if I have to."

Martha couldn't help but smirk as she continued.

"And you and I both know that because of your decision that day in the woods, this estate is anything but pure by you and your wife's standards. Life…God rather, always wins. Eventually, fear and evil loses. No matter how successful fear and evilness may be, they still end up losing. You lost everything worth having the day you hurt Hannah. Dignity, goodness, courage and compassion all departed from you that day. But that was your choice. You have chosen to live your life as a tyrant. And with every breath you take in this life, you lose. And deep down you know that is really why you hate others so much, especially the Lovemans. That is why you killed or permitted the killing of Benjamin and that is why now you are seeking to destroy

Gabriel. And you may succeed at that, but you will still lose. You will lose because no matter what happens to them, nothing you do can impose upon the beauty of Benjamin or the sheer brilliance of Gabriel. Benjamin's spirit lives on inside of his little brother. He may have died physically, but that glorious spirit lives on. I see him all the time. The presence of that wonderful man is in the smiles on the faces of the children I teach. It is in the strength of their mommas and daddies who love them even though they must labor so strenuously in your fields under your awful authority. I hear a song and Benjamin is there. I see a flower blossom or an apple tree in full bloom and Benjamin is there. And he lives on through Gabriel. Benjamin, more than anyone, knew how very special a human being Gabriel is and how extraordinary a life the one before him stands to be. You know it too, which is why you want to put a stop to it. Gabriel Loveman is everything you are not. He is a genius, albeit a very humble one, and he has never nor will he ever have to try to be anyone other than the man God created him to be. And he is loved by all who know him, including me, your twin sister and especially, spectacularly by your own seed, your one and only child, the daughter you will never acknowledge but who is Peterson blood as much as you and I."

Martha knew that, by speaking her brother's lifelong secret aloud, she was certain to awaken his deepest fear, which was certain to be accompanied by his aggravation and rage. She could see the anger in his eyes and his nostrils had begun to flare as soon as she referenced the child he had never acknowledged existed. Despite the immediate danger facing her, Martha knew she had to have what would probably be her final say with her twin.

"Ella, your child, loves Gabriel. Nothing you can do will ever change the love that surrounds him and that flows through him, whether he stays or goes. Everybody who knows him will always love Gabriel. Just as sure as nobody really loves you. Except me, maybe."

"You don't either." Robert replied in a huff.

Never before did he look as alone and pathetic as he did in that moment. Never before had Robert Peterson felt so small, so entirely worthless and empty. To hear his flesh and blood detail his life in a way that undermined everything he had convinced himself to believe about his wealth and his power had rattled him to his core. He was angry but more than that, he was sad. Still, he would never resort to acknowledging his true feelings and he refused to give Martha the satisfaction of knowing just how resound a chord she had struck in his conscious. He had tolerated as much of her honesty and clarity as he could stand and he already knew the hold she had on him, though he had never imagined that she would ever be bold, daring enough to ever stake her claim. Martha's display that day dictated otherwise, however, and she had made it painfully clear that she was not the mousy, weak woman he thought her to be. She obviously was capable of cruelty, for her words to him that day bore no love, no compassion. Just as he felt himself on the verge of giving into his sense of relief at the fact that maybe indeed she did still love him, Robert Peterson remembered himself. He had lived a life not needing love and he was not about to allow himself to give way to what he felt deep inside as she spoke. There comes a time in a wicked man's life, when he faces his demons or as in Robert Peterson's case is confronted about them, the time when he decides to admit to himself the outcomes of his evilness and his cowardice, the time when he can choose to accept who he really is as a human being and then and therefore allow his heart to be broken by that reality so that he can be forgiven and healed and made anew or when he can resign himself to his badness and move forward in hate and in rejection of love. Standing at that emotional crossroads, looking into the lovely and good and feminine version of himself, facing the very kind of human being he had lived his adult life refusing to be, Robert Peterson made his choice and when he spoke, the coward that dwelled within his spirit did all of the talking.

"I know you don't love me, that probably nobody does. What you don't seem to know is that I really don't give a damn. So you can save your sermon. I'm alright with the fact that I will more than likely spend eternity in hell. Might as well. That's where most everybody I know is anyway. But as long as I am breathing, I'd rather not waste another second on this shit you are talking about. So, Missy, why don't you just go ahead and tell me what you want. Get to the point of it all. I am sick of sitting here and I am sick of listening to you. Just go ahead and get to it, why don't you?"

For once, Martha agreed with her twin. Any time spent pleading to his conscience was a waste. Robert had no desire to be a better man and actually placed no value in goodness at all. He was destined to live all his years in the throes of his own wretched ways, the way he had since the day he had attempted to kill Hanna. Nothing she could do or say would change that. All he cared about was his wealth, his possessions and his standing among those who lived their lives in a fashion akin to his. To possibly accomplish what she so greatly desired, Martha would have to wager on the depth of her twin brother's devotion to his money and his reputation. The time had come to bring the matter to an end and to have her say once and for all. When she spoke again, she was emphatic.

"One of two things is going to happen when I leave here today. Either you are going to leave Gabriel and his family alone and continue to live out this miserable life of yours the way you wish, without any interference from me and when you die, this plantation will be inherited by your wife and her family, thereby remaining "pure." Except for the plots that hold the school and my house and those that house the Lovemans and Hanna and Ella, I will stake no claim. Everything will belong to you and Nancy, free from any demand on my part. Better yet, if Gabriel is left free to do as he so decides, once I know for certain he and his family and Ella and Hanna will suffer no harm at your hands, I will relinquish the claim I rightfully have and have always had on this entire estate."

Martha felt herself lowering to her knees in order to meet her twin brother eye to eye. She took a deep breath and placed both hands on Robert's face. She hadn't touched her brother in years. Surprisingly, he didn't pull away, not even as she made her final declaration.

"But should you act on the threat you made to Gabriel, if I hear of your attempt in any way to hurt Gabriel or his loved ones, including Ella and Hannah, especially Hannah and Ella, I will collapse your whole world. As a matter of fact, Brother, if you decide right now to strike me down, you will trigger your very own downfall. I knew when I came here today that I was putting my life on the line. But my life's no good anyway if I live out of the fear of being anything like you or if I live it ever again being afraid of what you will do to me-me, your own flesh and blood and the one person who somewhere deep down really does still love you. The only other person who truly loved you,you tried to kill, so I make myself no exception to the possibility of suffering your wrath. The difference in me and Hannah, my dear, pathetic Brother, is that with me, you had better finish the job, because if you don't, I will not run away. I will kill you. I will kill you without pause and with a glad heart. And even if you do kill me, I will still destroy you from my cold, dark grave. You remember I once had a beau myself, don't you? Well, he is now Senator and both he and my attorney have instructions for exactly what to do in the event of my disappearance or demise. And believe me, although I may not be alive to witness the outcome, I can imagine you will be made quite the public spectacle when all of society discovers who your daughter is and what she looks like. Everyone will know exactly how she ever even came to be. More than that they will know that she is a Peterson, and that this family is not purely white as you so proudly proclaim. And the half of this estate that is mine will become hers and there will be nothing you can do about it. "

With that, Martha stood and walked out of the parlor, down the long hallway, through the front door and away from her brother.

Chapter Twelve

LIFE AND LOVE

N ever before was there ever so little time between the closing of an evening and the breaking of the next day's dawn than the night before the day Gabriel had to make his decision, finally, one way or another. That night did not linger long and though Gabriel had not slept a wink, he was startled by the sun's first striking of light against his face. He had been awake most of the night, tossing and turning all of his matters over and over in his mind and the time was now upon him to accept what his deliberation had revealed. His chest cavity felt dull and heavy with remorse. As he sat up and reached for his shirt, he decided he should read the letter one last time before he laid the matter completely to rest both in his heart and in his mind.

At first Gabriel thought his sleepiness was getting in the way of his putting his hands on the acceptance letter right away. Maybe he was just hoping that his weariness was delaying his contact with the piece of paper that was usually within the quick reach of his fingers, but within a few seconds, Gabriel realized that the letter he had carried with him day in and day out, the document that he had not let out of his sight since first being placed in his hands by Robert Peterson, was not inside his shirt. When he first received the letter, he hadn't wanted to run the risk of his family coming across it, so rather than tuck it away in the corner of the cabin that was reserved for his privacy, Gabriel had always seen fit to keep the letter on his person. To keep the precious paper out of sight from others and perhaps more for the sake of his own comfort, the letter was placed in a pocket he had sewn inside his shirt solely for the purpose of storing what had quickly become his most prized possession. Whenever he had a moment to spare or some quiet time to himself, Gabriel would reach inside his shirt to the space close to his heart and retrieve his letter of acceptance to the University. Sometimes the words he read reassured him. Sometimes he was excited by the contents of the letter and sometimes he was frustrated by dilemma the message created in his life. Always, though, Gabriel was grateful, if for nothing else, for having the letter to hold in his hands, every now and again and to otherwise keep close to his heart. From the moment he had laid his eyes upon the letter, Gabriel had felt something he had not experienced since Benjamin's death. He felt hopeful. The letter had given him hope. Gabriel hadn't realized just how miserable, how hopeless his existence had been, until the letter had arrived and restored his optimism. His internal conflict over what to do had brought moments, hours, days even, when his hope, again, faded back almost to a state of non-existence, but the ability to simply reach inside his shirt for a quick rejuvenation of his spirit had kept him going through the mystery and the madness of his most fateful summer. And though nothing could ever replace the confidence and the safety that the relationship with Benjamin had given him every day of his life up until the very worst day of his life, the letter had somehow served as a comforting substitute.

With the letter in his hands or inside his shirt, next to his heart, Gabriel no longer felt the extreme loneliness caused by Benjamin's absence from his life. As much as he knew he had to move on past his grief over the death of his big brother, he also knew, given his decision to remain home, that he would have to stop relying on a piece of paper, a bunch of words, a written invitation to his imagined destiny to give him hope. And even though Gabriel had resolved to give up his dream of education and a life beyond the Peterson farmland, over the course of the summer, he had also realized how blessed he was to have the reasons for his decision. He loved his family and they needed him. And he loved Ella. More than he could ever explain, he more than loved Ella. He adored her. He hoped his decision would prove just how devoted he was to his love for her and he was even more hopeful that they would soon begin their life together. He also knew that although Ms. Martha would be disappointed by his decision, even she would understand and accept his fate. He, himself, had accepted his circumstances and, in Gabriel's mind, reading the letter one last time before he put it away for good would bring the matter to a close.

As resigned as he was, he still needed to read the letter once more so he could daydream about the possibilities acceptance to college created, finally and for good, before he started the day that would mirror most of the rest of his days to come on Peterson Plantation. Just one last time, Gabriel needed to keep company with his tangible hope. With closure as his mindset, he would read the letter, experience the hope and then let his dreams fade away. He needed to release himself from the hold the letter had on him if he had any chance of contentment, if there was to be any possibility of the existence of the letter making him better rather than the denial of the opportunity making him bitter. Still, before he could free himself entirely, now that his choice had been made, he wanted to read his letter, fly off in his balloon, for just a few minutes more before he began his new reality.

After fumbling around with his shirt for more than a few seconds, Gabriel allowed himself to accept that the letter was not there. His sleepy eyes quickly transformed from an early morning squint to the wide-eyed openness that accompanies feelings of shock and dismay. With the realization that the letter was not in his shirt pocket, Gabriel quickly dropped from his makeshift bed to his knees, hoping against hope that maybe the letter had somehow slid onto the floor below him. As he felt around the bare floor, Gabriel knew he would not find what he was looking for and his heart sank. The letter was gone. When he thought back over the day and the night before, he realized that he had been so caught up in the making of his final decision, he had not taken the letter out of his shirt pocket for at least a couple of days. Realizing that, more than likely, he had dropped the letter in the field or, even worse, under his great oak tree, where surely it had been taken up by a swift breeze, Gabriel was suddenly brought into the gut-wrenching reality of his decision. The letter was gone, as was his chance at the life his brilliance and his talents could produce, if only he had been born a different color, lived in a different part of the country or if only he was still the little brother to a living big brother who was ever so gracious and capable of taking care of their family.

The understanding rushed through his mind and settled in his heart and, without warning, Gabriel found himself on the floor doubled over by his acceptance of the loss of both Benjamin and his one and only chance to get away from the place and the people responsible for his brother's murder. He would have wailed, hollered or screamed if he could have, but the pain was so deep, so grappling, he could barely breathe. As the tears fell one after another, heavy drop by heavy drop, onto the floor beneath his knees, as he gasped for air, Gabriel gave in and, finally, finally, surrendered to his heartbreak.

From the moment that he had first heard the news of his brother's death to the moment when he had decided that foregoing an education and a move away from the Peterson Plantation was the best decision for him and his family, Gabriel had fought against his emotions. For the past few years and especially this summer, he had somehow convinced himself that crying would not do him, nor his situation, any good. He had trained himself to use his mind to consider his matters and with the exception of a few moments with Ella when he could not help but to let his guard down, Gabriel had gone for quite some time without hardly ever shedding a tear. In the early hours of the morning that could have been, that should have been, the dawn of a brand new day and a brand new life for him -then and there, on his knees, with the tears streaming steadily down his face-Gabriel broke the hold he maintained on his heartache and cried so hard his body shook all over. Once he began to cry, he couldn't imagine being able to stop the flow, for all of the tears he had withheld the past five years or so were released from the place in his soul where his sadness had been buried. Over the years, day after day, time and time again, Gabriel had struggled to contain his grief and to keep his emotions under control, for he felt certain that if he ever submitted to his sorrow, his whole life would be consumed with grief. If ever he cried, he thought, he would never be able to stop and would, thus, spend his life as a sad and pitiful man.

As Gabriel kneeled there, alone, by his bed, as the tears journeyed from somewhere inside his soul into his large, light brown eyes, and down and along his slender cheeks, he was amazed at how much he was overcome by an incredible sense of relief. Each tear seemed to carry a portion of the weight of his indecisiveness, his guilt, his frustration, and most importantly, his remorse and sadness. As his weeping resided and as his eyes began to dry, Gabriel realized that the very thing he had been holding onto, the very thing he had been determined to keep confined was the very thing he needed to give up. Even though he would always miss Benjamin and although he may spend his days ahead wondering about the life he could have had if he had decided to act on the letter, as he lifted his head up and prepared to stand, the sun lit up his tiny part of the cabin and Gabriel knew that all was well and that he could now live happily with his decision to stay and, yes, happily, in spite of the loss of the brother he loved so very much.

∞

Within moments of his resignation to remain and live his life with Ella and his family on the Peterson Plantation, Gabriel heard the horn that was blown every morning as a call to the fields. Knowing he only had a few minutes to refresh himself and eat whatever meager breakfast his Mother had prepared, he stepped onto the back porch, to use the wash basin and take in a few deep breaths of fresh morning air. He wanted no hint of the last night's tarrying to show on his face or in his demeanor. He had made his decision. His mind was settled and he was ready to face his future without regret. The last thing he wanted was for his family to bear any guilt or to carry any woe over the choice he had made and so Gabriel found himself all the more appreciative of his ability to keep the news of the letter from his family. Doing so had been much more difficult than he thought and if he had learned anything at all that summer, he had come to understand that he needed his family, his Mother, his Father and his Uncle just as much as they needed him. He decided right then and there that from that day on, he would be just as open with them as he was with Ella and Ms. Martha. They were all the loves of his life and being amongst them would be more than enough to give him as full a life as any man of color born in the south could ever expect to have.

Gabriel expected to see his parents and Uncle David when he walked back into the cabin and into the main room that housed the kitchen table and stove. They all usually gathered there every morning to pray and eat quickly before heading off to work in the fields. However, Gabriel did not expect them to be standing alongside one another awaiting his return from back porch and he did not expect his teacher to be standing inside the doorway to their cabin. Gabriel did not expect there to be a bundle of food wrapped tightly and tied to a stick for easy carrying on the table and he most certainly did not expect that bundle to be placed right next to his acceptance letter, the one he thought was lost to him forever.

No one said a word for a moment or two. Everyone knew that the table setting and Ms. Martha's presence pretty much made everything clear. As Gabriel turned his gaze from the eager faces of his loved ones to the contents of the kitchen table back to the faces of the family he loved so deeply, his knees buckled and his heart all but burst inside his chest cavity, as he stumbled toward the table in an effort to steady himself.

All kinds of thoughts began to race across his mind. How long had they known? When did they all decide that he would go? How would they manage in the fields without him? What about Robert Peterson? Would they be okay if he left? Would they be sad if he left? Would he be sad if he left? How could he leave them knowing he may never see them again?

Gabriel hadn't realized he was crying again until he felt his teacher's soft hand as she wiped away some of his tears. Just as Martha had known that she would have to push Gabriel to even apply to college, Martha Peterson was also keen enough to understand that he was the type of person who would always go out of his way to avoid troubling his loved ones with the decisions the acceptance letter would force him to make. Martha also knew that in the making of those decisions, Gabriel would be considerate of his family's sorrow and grief, so much so that he would make every effort to not worry them, especially over a threat from Robert Peterson. She was also wise enough to know that she had to divulge Gabriel's secret.

As much as she had involved herself in her favorite student's life, as much of her own time she had placed into cultivating his precious, rare intelligence, Martha knew that she was merely situated on the periphery of Gabriel's world. He was a Loveman and the Loveman Family was due the respect of having the same information as she did when it came to their son and nephew, Gabriel, the genius boy who had grown into a brilliant, admirable man she considered a friend, one of the only two she had. As anxious as Martha was for him to take advantage of the opportunity the letter availed to him, she appreciated the fact that the decision to be made was a family decision. When she first heard about the acceptance letter, with grave resolve, she had placed her trust in God and endeavored to breach Gabriel's confidence in her by sharing the news with his parents and uncle. Somehow, she knew that no matter the outcome, his family would support Gabriel's decision and always be there for him in any way possible.

When Martha relayed the contents of the letter to the Lovemans, she had explained the danger involved because of Robert Peterson's awareness of the whole matter and, thus, the heartbreaking decision on Gabriel's part to forego sharing his dilemma with them. When she left, the three of them had made a pact between themselves to table any more discussion about the letter while John and Rosalee took the time to think about the entire situation through and reach their own decision as to what they as a family should do about their darling boy's plight. Over the course of the summer, they had all been weighed down by the decision Gabriel had to make and they all shared the agony of being torn between excitement over the opportunity and torment over his possible departure. Standing in the kitchen facing his loved ones on the day that had preoccupied his mind for so long, Gabriel realized that as alone as he had felt, he had the company of his family all along that summer, in his both his optimism and in his misery over the offerings of the piece of paper that contained the pathway to his future.

A few days earlier, after Martha left her brother's house, she had gone straight to the Loveman's cabin. When she sat down with John, Rosalee and David, she had not minced her words. First, she informed them all of her earnest desire to see Gabriel leave the Peterson Plantation and how strongly she felt he would benefit remarkably from going to college. She had to admit that his safety and his removal from the South were equal drivers in her quest to see him go and though she knew they were aware of her affection toward Gabriel, Martha felt compelled to declare her love not just for him but for the entire Loveman family. And so, to earn their trust, she admitted to them what they already knew but would never say aloud – that she was Robert Peterson's twin and, thus, owner, of half of the estate where they lived and worked. She told them how she loved all the people of the Quarters but that she especially loved their family because of her connection with Gabriel and also because of her actual kinship with Ella, the young woman he loved and wanted to marry. Martha wanted the Lovemans to understand that all she did was for the both of them, that her dedication to, her fight for and her devotion to Gabriel was also an extension of her love and adoration for her niece, her twin brother's child.

Martha Peterson's verbal announcement of her biological relationship with Ella had serious implications. Every one, white, colored, rich or poor understood the high value society placed on the purity of the Peterson bloodline. Robert Peterson and his forefathers were known for not having ever fathered any children of color, which implied they had refrained from engaging in sexual contact with their slaves or sharecroppers. Not only were the Petersons wealthier than most families in Chester County, they were also morally superior to most all other white families, whose estates bore the proof of their indiscretions, as nothing made the sexual excursions of white men more obvious than the varying skin tones amongst the people of color living on their properties. The Peterson Family had not been humble when it came to their moral superiority in this regard. Robert Peterson's father, grandfather, and great-grandfather had all bragged as much and as often as possible about their unwillingness to taint what they considered to be the sanctity of their whiteness by having sex with their female slaves or the descendants of those slaves. The birthing of countless interracial children in the South was a taboo subject but though prescriptive in nature, conversations still occurred, mostly within the confines of taverns and back rooms and in the secrecy of the society of white men only. In those close circles, the Peterson family was infamous for making reference to their heightened social status by reminding neighbors, church members, business partners, politicians and anyone they were seeking to influence or intimidate of their purity and sanctification.

Martha's admission that Ella was actually the child born as a result of her brother's raping of her childhood friend stood to destroy the entire Peterson financial dynasty. Robert Peterson had killed for much more trivial reasons and as confident as Martha was that her threat against him would work, everyone knew that the man was evil enough, powerful enough to bring about the death of them all, including his own sister. Even with Martha's entrustment of the matter with her former beau, there was no guarantee that Robert Peterson would concede. They all agreed that, if ever a person, a matter, a dream, a vision, a hope was worth the risk, the one before them was deserving of them all placing everything on the line.

And so the four of them had worked it all out. Martha Peterson took the next few days to make the travel arrangements and to settle all of the financial requirements necessary to allow Gabriel to focus on his studies without having to worry about money for food and shelter. His family took on the task of communicating what needed to happen in order for Gabriel to go to Ella and her family. The conversation was deliberate and heart-wrenching but both families agreed that the right thing was for Gabriel to exercise his genius far and away from the Peterson Plantation. They all agreed that love is sacrificial and that the time had come to show their love for Gabriel. Ella surprised herself when she agreed with his family and when she made the ultimate sacrifice out of her love for Gabriel. Her Mother and her Aunt had promised to support her for the rest of their lives and she also knew that the Lovemans considered her as one of their own and that, no matter what, they always would be there for her, as much as they were for Gabriel.

∞

That morning, the day that he would have to leave if he was going to go, Gabriel knew from the look in his family's eyes there was little left to say. He took a couple of minutes to let his family's stance sink in before he lifted his head and simply said, "Thank y'all."

As the tears streamed down his face, he retrieved his letter of acceptance from the kitchen table and, once again, placed it on the inside of his shirt. He then pulled on the tattered jacket that was also there with the other things his family had prepared for him. God only knew who had offered the coat in support of his departure and there was no time for Gabriel to even ask. He had to get moving before he or any of them lost the courage needed to let him go. As he collected his belongings from the table, a hush fell over the room as they all became profoundly aware of what was actually taking place. Gabriel Loveman was leaving the Peterson Plantation, leaving Chester County and leaving them all, with no guarantee of return.

His Uncle David, a man known to never be short on his words, had little to say as he reached out and embraced his nephew, kissing both of Gabriel's cheeks, as he instructed, "Do us proud, Young Blood. You always have and, well, anyways, I know you always will." Then pulling away and drawing a deep breath to stifle his sadness, for he so wanted to send the boy off in high spirits, David sought to reassure Gabriel that everything would be alright, after he left. "And don't worry about us," he urged. "That ole' Mista Robert done caught the Holy Ghost or done run face to face with the devil he scared to share hell with and came around here yesterday and told your Ma and Pa that all they debts is paid and done even gave your Daddy the title to the property and told him to file it at the courthouse if he wanna. Even said we don't have to worry about food, if we fall a little short. Yeah. That man must've went a little bit crazy in the head, too, because he done gave me a deed to the property he took from me years ago when I moved in here with y'all. With a little property, I might have to follow your lead, Nephew, and start courting Hanna. What you say, huh? You got to think that's a good idea!" David insisted, doing his best to place as much lightness in his voice as possible.

Gabriel just shook his head, thinking it was just like his Uncle David to send him off with a laugh. As he turned to his mother, suddenly Gabriel felt boyish and his heart began to race. Grabbing her waist as he placed a small amount of space between the two of them, he looked Rosalee squarely in the eyes, as he inquired, "Momma, will you be okay if I leave? Do you promise you are alright with this?"

Even the slightest suggestion by Rosalee that she could not bear him leaving would keep Gabriel from going. Everyone in the room knew that, Rosalee most of all. As she stood before her youngest boy and only living child, Rosalee knew that all her grief and sorrow had brought her to this moment. Every painful moment seemed to now be replaced with a sense of accomplishment and joy. She had been placed on Earth to give birth to Benjamin and to Gabriel. One had been taken, brutally and without her say. His death had almost destroyed her. Gabriel had been her saving grace and as she looked into his eyes, large, looming eyes, filled with eagerness and concern, Rosalee knew she would now return that grace. Her heart filled with love and excitement, as she responded.

"I am fine with this, baby. More than fine. This here is my dream coming true right before my eyes. This done made me happy and I didn't think I was ever gone be happy again. I am now." Rosalee nodded as to convince Gabriel that she meant every single word she said, because she truly wanted him to know how certain she was that he should go. She knew her son needed the push that only a mother can give and so she continued, refusing to cry and relishing in her last few minutes with her baby boy.

"You got to get going, Son. You got to travel. But just know, you gone still be with me. I got your love and it don't travel, baby. Your love stays right here with me and you take mines with you."

Pulling Gabriel in as tightly as she could, she whispered her parting words into her darling boy's ear. "You give me such good love, child. You are your mother's joy."

And then she released him from her grasp in the way only a loving mother can, the way that says to a child that he must move forward and never look back in regret.

Witnessing Gabriel's last moments with his family had torn at Martha's heart in a way that she had not expected. She had been detached from her own family for so long she had forgotten the preciousness of blood relation. She had been so determined to see this day, so busy figuring out a way to help Gabriel accomplish his dream of higher learning, Martha had also failed to consider how sad she was going to be to see him actually leave. Indeed, she was going to miss him, not because he was such a brilliant student but because he was the best person she had ever known, the best heart she had ever encountered and no one, as far as she was concerned, deserved happiness more than him, no one except maybe her beloved Ella.

As if he read her mind, Gabriel turned to Martha and asked, nervously, "Where's Ella? Does she know about this?"

His voice became a bit hoarse and his words were hurried, as he realized Ella's absence and began to worry that he would not see her before he left.

"I need to talk to her before I go. I can't just leave without seeing her. I need to explain to her what is happening. I..."

Martha put her hand to Gabriel's mouth to interrupt his rant. Placing her hand gently on his shoulder, she spoke clearly and with calmness.

"Hush now. There is no need for you to worry about that. She already knows you are leaving today. We all talked to her and she is more than fine with it. Besides, you can't talk to her before you leave, anyway, because she's not here."

Gabriel pulled away from his teacher to inquire about his love's whereabouts, but Martha reached for him again and held him by both shoulders, as she explained.

"She's not here because she left yesterday and she will be there when you arrive. She is boarding with a dear friend of mine and his family. They live very near the University you will be attending and very near the school for colored children where Ella is set to begin teaching in a couple of weeks."

Gabriel knew that Martha was responsible for much of what was occurring and as he looked into the lovely face of the only white person he really knew, his heart filled with love and gratitude for all she had done for him and Ella and his family. He knew that she had orchestrated both his and Ella's safe departure and that her doing so had been no small feat. Gabriel also knew that she had provided the money for his room and board and train fare. The little money his parents and Uncle could spare was folded neatly and securely placed in the knapsack that was still sitting on the table. As he gathered the bag that held his money and the food packed for his trip, Gabriel insisted softly, "I don't know how I will ever be able to repay you for all you have done for me, Ms. Martha."

Her heart sank at his declaration of gratefulness. Martha had never known a more humble soul. She knew that whatever was to become of Gabriel Loveman, he would go through life with his humility in tact. He was destined to become someone magnificent, indeed. As she looked upon her favorite person, Martha was overcome with thankfulness, herself, for he was already so excellent at being human, she could bid him goodbye with no worry and no regret. More than that, she could wish him well, all the while feeling grateful that he had been such a vital part of her life the past eighteen years. She kissed him on the cheek as she patted his shoulder and tilted her head toward the door in an effort to get him moving along.

"Your happiness and your success is all the repayment I need. Besides your going is just as much for me as it is for you. Gabriel,..."

Martha paused and caught her breath which had suddenly been made short by the gravity of him leaving. Wanting desperately to bid him farewell in as upbeat a manner as she could display, Martha braced herself, straightened her back and instructed her beloved student one last time.

"Keep in touch, please. I'll miss you. I will miss you so."

Gabriel knew he was running out of time and that he could not linger much longer. Instead of saying goodbye to his teacher, his mentor, his best friend, he just smiled and replied, "I will miss you, too, but I promise I will write often."

There was only one person left for Gabriel to bid goodbye before he left the cabin that housed the family he loved with all his heart. Moments before, John had walked out onto the porch, for the sight of Gabriel saying goodbye to Rosalee had been more than he could bear to watch. Gabriel knew that his departure was hurting his father more than words could say. Besides, John was a man of dignity, a man not often prone to any display of emotion, no matter how deeply he felt. Gabriel knew that, by walking away, his father was fighting the urge to weep, for, again, he was losing another son, not to death, but to distance. When he walked out onto the porch, Gabriel could also sense John's sadness. And so, without a word, after hugging his mother, his uncle, and his teacher one last time, Gabriel slowly walked past his father, stopping at the man's side only for the few seconds it took to place a hand upon John's face, silently saying goodbye to his father with a loving pat on John's wrinkled cheek, which was wet with tears. As he trotted down the steps and began to walk the path that would take him away from the Peterson Plantation and away from his family, perhaps for good, Gabriel did not look back.

A few steps beyond the porch and just as he swung the knapsack over his shoulder and straightened himself all the way up, just when Gabriel began his walk toward the boundary line between the Peterson Plantation and the rest of the world, he was reassured of his father's approval and reminded of his unconditional love, when he heard John begin to sing. Gabriel Loveman then left the Peterson Plantation and entered his new life with his favorite song hovering over his head and with the melody settling forever into his heart....

I was sinking deep in sin
Far from the peaceful shore
Very deeply stained within
Sinking to rise no more
But the Master of the sea
Heard my despairing cry
And from the waters lifted me
Now safe am I

Love lifted me (even me)
Love lifted me (even me)
When nothing else could help
Love lifted me.

The End (And the Beginning.)

ACKNOWLEDGEMENTS

I thank God for allowing me to write this book and for each and every blessing bestowed upon my life. Indeed, I am blessed with God's divine love and the grace that is necessary for the best nurturing of a writer's soul and the best protection of a writer's mind.

Daddy, my Angel, thank you for understanding the way my mind works and for investing in my love affair with books. You were the one who first required my mastery of the English language and I am so grateful I had a Daddy as brilliant as you. I miss you everyday. I place your grin on Gabriel's face. He reminds me of you. Your love lifts me.

Momma, thank you for staying the course and for being my shelter. You have always created that safe space I need to just be myself and you have refused to allow me to give up on my dreams. Thank you for being my closest friend. No one believes in me as faithfully as you do. I could create Rosalee because you showed me who to write. Your love fuels me.

Bradley, thank you for loving me for who I am, flaws and all. Only the best of hearts can love a writer day to day. Courageous is the soul that dares to spend this life with one who spends hours on end putting pen to paper. Thank you for never allowing doubt and frustration to win me over and for the careful way you require me to be brave. Your love keeps me.

To my brothers, Jeffery and Maurice, thank you both for your love and support. I always say Jeff is the most artistic of the three of us and Maurice is the most intelligent and that I fall in the middle of the two. I will always hold down the middle. Your love inspires me.

Shelby, thank you so much. You were the first of my Sister-Friends and you have taught me how to take quantum leaps of faith and how to be a loyal friend. You have walked alongside me from the inception and tolerated the craziest of notions as if they were the most ordinary of thoughts. I will always appreciate how much you have believed in this vision. Thank you for always making room for me and for being there for each and every chapter of my life.

There are so many loved ones who have supported me along the way. You know who you are and I know in my heart that I could not have completed this book without your love and encouragement. I have to especially acknowledge Deena, Sheri and Sandra for their gracious and in-depth editorial input. I also have to say how much I cherish and appreciate my best friend James N. and my other Sister-Friends, who have all been so supportive- April, Vetta, Michelle, Sadiqa, Kimberly, Monica, Valarie, Angela C., Patsy, Brigitte, Caiphia, Sherry S., Patricia, Tessie, Shemmie, Carmen, Ericka, Shayla, Sheila, Sherry P. and Angela B.

CPSIA information can be obtained
at www.ICGtesting.com
Printed in the USA
JSHW011027271219
3225JS00002B/8